Someone To Watch Over Her

"I, of course, am Connor Gibbs. You, I presume, are Ms. Chevalier."

"Leontine Chevalier."

"Beautiful name. Uncommon."

"I'll say."

"And what can I do to help you?" asked Gibbs, very tall, very thick, very direct.

The woman said abruptly, "I'm impulsive."

"Too many shoes in the closet?"

"Not about shopping," she snapped impatiently, a brief glimpse of her nature, hurriedly corrected. "Something much more serious, I'm afraid."

Connor waited. In vain. "I'm not a seer, Ms. Chevalier," he prompted.

She drew in a huge draft of office air, let out half, and plunged: "I need you to keep me from killing a man."

MORE MYSTERIES FROM THE
BERKLEY PUBLISHING GROUP . . .

THE HERON CARVIC MISS SEETON MYSTERIES: Retired art teacher Miss Seeton steps in where Scotland Yard stumbles. "A most beguiling protagonist!"

—*New York Times*

by Heron Carvic
MISS SEETON SINGS
MISS SEETON DRAWS THE LINE
WITCH MISS SEETON
PICTURE MISS SEETON
ODDS ON MISS SEETON

by Hampton Charles
ADVANTAGE MISS SEETON
MISS SEETON AT THE HELM
MISS SEETON, BY APPOINTMENT

by Hamilton Crane
HANDS UP, MISS SEETON
MISS SEETON CRACKS THE CASE
MISS SEETON PAINTS THE TOWN
MISS SEETON BY MOONLIGHT
MISS SEETON ROCKS THE CRADLE
MISS SEETON GOES TO BAT
MISS SEETON PLANTS SUSPICION
STARRING MISS SEETON
MISS SEETON UNDERCOVER
MISS SEETON RULES
SOLD TO MISS SEETON
SWEET MISS SEETON
BONJOUR, MISS SEETON
MISS SEETON'S FINEST HOUR

KATE SHUGAK MYSTERIES: A former D.A. solves crimes in the far Alaska north . . .

by Dana Stabenow
A COLD DAY FOR MURDER
DEAD IN THE WATER
A FATAL THAW
BREAKUP
A COLD-BLOODED BUSINESS

PLAY WITH FIRE
BLOOD WILL TELL
KILLING GROUNDS
HUNTER'S MOON

INSPECTOR BANKS MYSTERIES: Award-winning British detective fiction at its finest . . . "Robinson's novels are habit-forming!"

—*West Coast Review of Books*

by Peter Robinson
THE HANGING VALLEY
WEDNESDAY'S CHILD
INNOCENT GRAVES

PAST REASON HATED
FINAL ACCOUNT
GALLOWS VIEW

CASS JAMESON MYSTERIES: Lawyer Cass Jameson seeks justice in the criminal courts of New York City in this highly acclaimed series . . . "A witty, gritty heroine."

—*New York Post*

by Carolyn Wheat
FRESH KILLS
MEAN STREAK
TROUBLED WATERS

DEAD MAN'S THOUGHTS
WHERE NOBODY DIES
SWORN TO DEFEND

JACK McMORROW MYSTERIES: The highly acclaimed series set in a Maine mill town and starring a newspaperman with a knack for crime solving . . . "Gerry Boyle is the genuine article."

—*Robert B. Parker*

by Gerry Boyle
DEADLINE
LIFELINE
BORDERLINE

BLOODLINE
POTSHOT
COVER STORY

Play
Dead

Leo Atkins

BERKLEY PRIME CRIME, NEW YORK

PLAY DEAD

A Berkley Prime Crime Book / published by arrangement with the author

PRINTING HISTORY
Berkley Prime Crime mass-market edition / March 2000

The Penguin Putnam Inc. World Wide Web site address is
http://www.penguinputnam.com

ISBN: 0-425-17362-3

Berkley Prime Crime Books are published
by The Berkley Publishing Group,
a division of Penguin Putnam Inc.,
375 Hudson Street, New York, New York 10014.
The name BERKLEY PRIME CRIME and the BERKLEY PRIME CRIME
design are trademarks belonging to Penguin Putnam Inc.

PRINTED IN THE UNITED STATES OF AMERICA

10 9 8 7 6 5 4 3 2 1

To Emma Lee Laine, an angel in teacher's guise

Acknowledgments:

As always, my son Christopher, about to turn twelve as this book goes to print, smarter and more talented than I in every way. Just not as good looking.

Wanda Faye Hiatt, dear to my heart of hearts.

Anne Tyler Ashley, my elder sister, who reared four kids single-handedly, good-naturedly, and without raising her voice. Right.

Nancy Fleming, the Pennsylvania pixie who reads everything that pops out of this machine, usually when it's hot off the roller. A gem, Miss Nancy.

Mike Holloway, father, husband, friend. None better.

Ed Humburg, devoted parent, master of innuendo, lover of forests, knocker of miscreant heads, as needed.

Ruby Hawks, who reads everything, and knows what she likes.

Pal Andy Riedell, whose true stories demean my feeble attempts.

Galen Hobbs, writer, host of hosts, who sets up a mean crab scrimmage; Sharon and Keith Hartung, a divine match; CarlaGay Higgins, author, and her husband Michael, wit; Andrea Young, whose snowflakes sigh; Marj Zepernick, who doesn't like to write on demand, but can; Martha Howell, who, after a forty-year hiatus, is again taking up the quill.

Tom Colgan, an editor's editor. No matter what he claims, I do *not* drive him crazy. (I drive Samantha crazy.)

Seth Robertson, agent in training who does what he says he'll do, rare in this racket. Maybe any racket.

And Jelly Bean, undoubtedly leaving hair on something as I key this in. She's a joy, but don't tell her I said so. It'll only encourage her.

Play
Dead

Prologue

Wind tugged at his curly hair as he strolled. "Three little monkeys, sitting in a tree . . . ," he sang aloud, his off-brand shoes from Family Dollar scuffing the dirt road; his mama couldn't afford better, not now with Big Sam gone. "Along came Mister Alligator, quiet as can be . . ." His voice, lofted by the breeze, continued, pleasant and free-spirited.

A quarter mile away, an ear cocked. Two. Four. The remains of a rabbit, now ignored, dropped into the ditch. Road dust, stirred by scurrying legs, drifted listlessly on the breeze.

Eddie Chevalier looked back over his shoulder, toward the security of the trailer park from which his mama had just hustled him on his way to the store. *Prob'ly washing the baby right now,* he thought. *She's always fussing over him.* Well, that was just fine by Eddie, who Mama loved the most, anyway, because he looked just like his daddy, Big Sam, killed in a motorcycle accident six months before the new baby was born. A tear tracked his cheek as Eddie Chevalier—now the man of the house, seven years old and counting—stopped, turned, stood gazing homeward, toward his mama, his brother, the tire swing he played on daily, there not being much else to do, what with no kids his age in the park.

Something huge slammed into him from behind, bowling him over like a straw figure. He yelled once in surprise, then grunted in pain as a pair of jaws clamped hard onto his right thigh, high at the rear. A second slavering faceful of teeth lunged at his chest, but he instinctively deflected the threat with a forearm. Mama had always told him it was no use running from a dog because the dog could always run faster than he could. Instead, she'd advised ramming a fist down the animal's throat, the theory being that while the dog was chewing on an arm it couldn't be chewing on something vital.

Under the tight stricture of panic, the boy vetoed his mama's advice. When the dog in front tried for his chest again, Eddie jammed a stiffened index finger into its eye, spun and kicked miraculously free of the other animal, then jumped, over and down—into the ditch beside the road— and then scampered squirrel-like up a tall bordering chain-link fence.

In vain.

He fell off.

But the dogs, hampered by the steep slope of the ditch, were laggard in their pursuit, giving Eddie time to regain his precarious perch.

And there he stayed, 'til dark—pained and bleeding, but clinging like a sandspur—until the dogs tired of the game and departed.

They took one of his shoes with them. It had much blood on it.

Two Days Later

Pale, papery skin surrounded hollow eyes with deep purple folds beneath, but the gaze was clear enough, and purposeful. "I need a dog," she said. "My husband died a few months back, and then . . ." Her voice trailed off. The eyes, though, never wavered. Inhaling a deep, bolstering draft, she continued. "I want something to care for."

Ginny Lambreth, portly and pink, nodded. "I understand, dear," she proffered in her auntly way. "Something small? We have the cutest little terrier mix. His name—"

"No!" objected the thin woman, her hands twisting at a baggy purse, attitude insistent. "I want one for protection, too. You got any of those big black and brown ones, like in the movies? I can't remember the name."

"We got big dogs, all right, not to mention middle-size," Ginny said, and started walking, the slender woman falling in behind, clinging to the purse and taking in her surroundings, head up, alert, moving like a ballerina on the balls of her feet. Ms. Lambreth prattled about a clutch of collie/springer puppies "adorable enough to eat" as they moved through a pair of swinging doors, down a corridor reeking of disinfectant, dogleg to the left, mauve walls in need of paint, then through a metal door with a big stainless-steel knob and a grated window, into a concrete-floored room filled with panting mutts in cages, hundred-pound sacks of Gravy Train, and the steamy odor of canine excreta.

"Right over here, Ms. . . . what'd you say your name was?" Ginny asked. The pale woman had paused near a padlocked cage and stood staring at a pair of very large animals. The animals, undaunted by the scrutiny, stared back.

Ginny bustled over and took hold of a slender arm, saying, "C'mon, dear. Those aren't for adoption."

"What kind are they?" asked the gaunt woman, resisting Ginny's tug.

"Doesn't matter. They're not going anywhere. Not for a while, at least," she muttered as if in afterthought.

"Why not?"

Ginny Lambreth glanced down the hall, then back over her shoulder. Bending close, she said, "Those two attacked a little boy last week. They're here for rabies observation."

With no change of expression at all, the thin woman

replied, "Really. Well then, how about that one over there?" She pointed with her chin.

When Ginny Lambreth turned to look in the direction indicated, the thin woman's hand dipped into the oversized purse and came out with a small black revolver. Poking its stubby barrel through the bars of the cage, she shot the nearest rottweiler between the eyes, spraying bloody gray matter all over the wall. When the second dog growled deep in its throat and launched itself at the bars, the pale woman shot it four times in the chest, her last bullet breaking a shoulder and dumping the beast at her feet, its quivering nose extending through the bars, teeth snapping in ire and frustration.

The dog died an hour later, despite the best efforts of an on-call veterinarian.

Three Days Later

"And so you blamed the dogs?" questioned the lawyer, his chin resting on the tips of dark, steepled fingers. He was sartorially splendid and redolent of Brut.

"No, I blame the bastard who owns them," said the thin pale woman, who wore an inexpensive blue dress and no perfume.

"And who's that?"

"Man by the name of Gantt Helms."

Oh shit, thought the lawyer, whose name was Holmes Crenshaw, but what he said was, "And you want me to defend you on the weapons charge?"

"No. I want you to find out everything you know about this Helms character."

"Why? You plan to sue?"

"Sue? Hell no. I plan to put him in the ground."

Chapter I

THERE WAS SLEET ON THE GROUND, AND SNOW, but inside, glowing with warmth from the fireplace, sat Cody Wainwright McGraw, often known as Blister. In his hand, cocoa; in his ear, music, seasonal music, and he was saying, "I've never heard a Christmas song that made me want to dance." Blister was nine and couldn't dance a lick, not for lack of trying but lack of rhythm.

Across the spacious office sat Connor Gibbs, leaning back with his feet up on his desk and a toddy nearby. "I have Cameron on video doing a jig to that very tune," he replied somberly. "He was three, maybe four. Cute as a button," staring into the fire.

The tune under discussion was "God Rest Ye Merry, Gentlemen," Mannheim Steamroller version, its undulating bonhomie filling the room, courtesy of a six-speaker surround system. Gibbs's office was sparsely furnished and currently dark, lit only by the fire and Blister's good will. A ten-foot Fraser fir graced a corner, gaily bedecked but lightless so as not to compete with the cheery fire.

Blister gazed at the tree, uncertain of his course. Conversation about Connor's son tended to make the big man morose. "How many of those decorations did Cameron make, or paint, or whatever?" he tried.

Gibbs reduced his toddy by a third and licked his lips. "Probably half. He loved doing them."

"Does he still?"

More toddy down the pipe. "Who knows?"

Blister abandoned tack; his friend's pain was especially obvious tonight. To safer ground: "Who's this lady we're waiting for?"

"Name's Chevalier, according to Holmie," Gibbs responded, thankful for the subject shift.

"She want you to find someone, like I did when I first met you?"

"Holmes was spare with the details, as is his habit when he's in a hurry. Just said she needed help and was coming by."

"You'll help anybody, won't you?"

"Except Latrell Sprewell."

"Who's that?"

"The grinch who choked Christmas."

And then the office door opened.

Chapter 2

"I HEAR YOU, UM, ASSIST PEOPLE," SHE SAID, standing in the open doorway, tall and straight, and epitomizing the word "gaunt." Determined, though, with a resolute jaw and clear eyes that looked right into you.

"When I can," Gibbs replied, feet coming off the desk. Blister stood as well, awkwardly, scurrying to quell Mannheim. The woman's eyes twinkled in the firelight. "Glad to see that some gentlemen still rise for a lady." She glanced at the ceiling fixture. "Forget to pay the electric?"

Gibbs crossed the room to flip a switch. Light flooded, and the shadows were less threatening. "Take your coat?" he asked.

"Just don't forget where you got it," she replied, shrugging out of it as he reached a huge hand.

"No problem. It's not my size," he responded in kind.

She smiled crookedly. "That's for sure. You're a big one."

Connor took the damp garment to a coatrack, saying "Have a seat" as he walked. Then, "Would you like some cocoa?"

"No thanks," she demurred, settling onto the client's chair, her slender head swiveling to take in the room: bust of

Jackie Robinson, garnished with a festive red bow; bejeweled Christmas tree; many framed photos of a child in various stages and ages and garb. "Those pictures are not of your partner here," she observed.

Gibbs resat and said, "Correct. By the way, this stalwart young man is Cody McGraw, but call him Blister."

"Blister?"

"It's a long story," said the stalwart young man. "I'm pleased to meet you."

"Me too," she said.

"I, of course, am Connor Gibbs," said Connor Gibbs. "You, I presume, are Ms. Chevalier."

"Leontine Chevalier," she amended.

"Beautiful name. Uncommon."

"I'll say. My mother read it in a book once, when she was pregnant. So here I am."

"And what can I do to help you?" asked Gibbs, very tall, very thick, very direct, azure- eyed, and open-minded.

"Mr. Crenshaw didn't explain my predicament?"

"Not a clue."

While the lady feigned ambivalence, Blister went to the tree and plugged in its rope of lights, multicolored, and the brilliant angel at the crest. Gilt ornaments refracted the lights willy-nilly. The boy cocked his head to admire the effect, then took his seat and tended to his cocoa.

The woman said abruptly, "I'm impulsive."

Gibbs nodded encouragingly. "Too many shoes in the closet?" he said.

"Not about shopping," she snapped impatiently, a brief glimpse of her nature, hurriedly corrected. "Something much more serious, I'm afraid."

Connor waited. Naught else was forthcoming. "I'm not a seer, Ms. Chevalier," he prompted.

She drew in a huge draft of office air, let out half, and plunged: "I need you to keep me from killing a man."

Tick of clock, groan of radiator, sounds of the aged building settling. Early evening traffic below; a horn honking somewhere. Up the alley, a trash can rattled. Leontine Eudora Chevalier was a real conversation stopper.

Blister's cocoa was forgotten, but Connor tossed off his toddy and said, "Who do you plan to kill and why?"

Another draft, another plunge. "Let's start at the beginning," she began.

He nodded. "A logical place."

"Six months ago, a child was killed while standing in line for a school bus. Three pit bulls tore him to shreds in front of sixteen frightened, howling kids."

A nod from Gibbs, a burble of nausea within young McGraw.

"Those dogs belonged to a slug named Gantt Helms."

Another Gibbs nod.

"He claimed they dug under the fence and ran amuck."

"Good choice of words."

"The dogs were caught and put to sleep."

"I remember." Gibbs's head was tired of bobbing.

"Nothing was done to Helms."

Gibbs arched his brows for variety, as in "Go on."

She did. "Ten days ago, my boy Eddie was attacked by a pair of rottweilers."

Aha.

"He wasn't killed, but he was chewed up pretty bad, especially one leg. There went his figure-skating career."

Gibbs, having paid careful attention, began to skip ahead.

"If Eddie hadn't climbed a fence," Leontine continued, "he probably would have been ripped to shreds."

"I read about it in the paper. Those dogs also belonged to Helms, if memory serves," Connor interjected.

"You get a prize."

"And two days later you splattered those dogs all over the animal shelter with a handgun."

"I sure did."

"And were subsequently arrested for discharging a firearm within the city limits and reckless endangerment."

"I sure was."

"Might I presume that the man you wish to shoot is the negligent Mr. Helms?"

"You sure can."

"Well now."

"Will you help me?"

"Shoot him?"

"No. Hold him so I can shoot him. Of course not, Mr. Gibbs. Help me *not* shoot him."

"How?"

"Move in with me. Keep an eye on me, just for a while. Help me resist my compulsion."

"Move in, huh? No hanky-panky, now."

Not even a trace of a smile. "Absolutely none."

"Aw, heck." He grinned broadly. "Did you drive over?"

She shook her head. "Cab. My transportation is on the fritz. Besides, I hate to drive in the snow."

"Goody," said Connor. "I get to drive, and me just getting my license back, too."

Through a look of mild alarm, she asked, "How did you lose your license?"

"Speeding."

Blister, collecting cups—his and Gibbs's—for deposit in the bathroom sink, just shook his head.

Leontine said, "How fast were you going?"

"Not very fast," Connor averred.

Blister smiled to himself. *Here it comes.*

"*How* fast?"

Gibbs could do sheepish quite convincingly, and did so now. "Oh, about a hundred. In a hospital zone. I told you it wasn't very fast, but, man, did those wheelchairs scatter."

She was aghast.

Blister, back from the lavatory, took Leontine's hand.

"Don't worry, Ms. Chevalier, if my Aunt Vera lets me ride with him, he's plenty safe. Connor's pulling your leg."

"Oh," she said, one hand at her throat, obviously relieved. "How can you tell?"

"You get to know him."

"Then you can tell?"

"About half the time."

"What about the other half?"

Blister shrugged. "He does keep you guessing."

"Never a dull moment," Gibbs allowed and ushered his charges into the clinging cold.

Chapter 3

A CARPET OF WHITE NOW, SUSAN B. ANTHONY-sized flakes falling as Gibbs piloted his passengers toward the outskirts of town. Blister was talking Ms. Chevalier's ear off from the backseat. Dodging a fender-bender, Connor punched a number into his cell phone.

"Sur, Arthur, Cone, and Doyle. How may I help you?" came Laverne's voice, polite, melodious, and mildly coarsened from years with tobacco.

"Put the barrister on."

"That you, Connor?"

"Jimmy Hoffa."

"Yeah? Where you calling from, Jimmy?"

"Can't say. Elvis wouldn't like it."

"I should care, me who never lusted after him even when I was young and full of nubility?"

"You're as nubile as ever, Laverne."

"All two hundred pounds of me?"

"More to love. Besides, that's not too much more than Bennie tips the beam."

"Yeah, but Benella, God bless her, is over six feet tall."

"Only barefoot. In shoes, she's five-feet-two. By the way, why're you working so late?"

"I need the overtime. Lots of stockings to fill."

"How many kids is it?"

"Six, but who's counting. Let me see if Mr. Crenshaw can spare a minute. Wait right there, you big galoot," she ordered, poking a button. Then Julie Andrews filled Connor's ear, midway through "Hark, the Herald Angels Sing."

Julie went away as abruptly as she'd appeared. "What's up, *sufi?*" Crenshaw greeted, just as if he didn't know.

"What are you doing to me, Holmes?" Connor said *sotto voce.*

"Ms. Chevalier?"

"You know damn well."

"What's the prob?"

"Prob*lem,* you're not sixteen. Except behaviorally. The problem is that this one stirs up memories, none good."

Having anticipated this, Holmes sat on his response for a moment, a courtroom ploy he often used. "She needs help, pal. I'm seriously afraid she might do the dogs' owner, and she's got a spanking new baby boy, and no local family. Where'd that leave him, not to mention Eddie?"

No response from Connor.

"You still there?" Holmes prodded.

"What's Gantt's excuse?" Gibbs asked.

"Claims the dogs dug under the fence."

"Again?"

"What can I say?"

"The mere possibility of that happening twice would seem to indicate negligence."

"Woulda, shoulda, coulda. Means little in a court of law. Oh, I'll sue the bastard, pro bono, on Eddie's behalf. But Connor, old chum, the family won't get much if Helms is *dead.*"

"You think she really might pop him?"

"Don't you? Hell, she blew those dogs away right in front of everybody."

Gibbs pondered briefly, then sighed into his end of the connection. "I suppose she might at that."

"That why you agreed to help her?"

"Who says I agreed?"

Holmes snorted. "Why am I still talking to you? I have work to do, for paying clients like Braxton Chiles."

"What's Chiles into now?"

"Tell you later." And they rang off.

"I'm causing you grief," said Leontine Chevalier from the backseat.

"Nothing I can't handle. Besides, you need help," from Gibbs. "Gantt Helms is bad business."

"And Connor's help is the best help there is," vouched Blister, taking in the decorative Christmas lights as they negotiated a housing development.

They motored on in the increasing thickness, reduced visibility cocooning them on every side. At the McGraw house—which seemed to leap suddenly at them from the crystal murk—Gibbs slid to a precarious halt. "My best to Vera," he said as Blister leaned forward to give him a peck on the cheek.

"Why don't you stay with us?" said the boy. "There's plenty of room and—"

Connor caressed the child's face with a calloused hand. "I'll be okay. Thanks, though."

"Call when you get home?"

"I will," Connor reassured.

"Promise?"

"You bet."

Blister kissed him again and was gone, engulfed by swirling flakes.

Not often you see a boy that age kiss a man, thought Leontine, as Connor slipped into gear and spun away from the curb.

She directed him to her mobile home park, asked him in—politely declined—then said, "When can you come stay?"

"Tomorrow. I'll pack tonight, pick you up for supper tomorrow afternoon. Think you can go one day without gunning Helms down?"

"Who says I don't plan to bomb him?"

"You don't seem the explosives kind, plus I suspect the collateral damage would bother you. Bombs are messy and indiscriminate."

"Maybe I'll poison him."

"You'd never get that close."

"Who is this guy?"

"A very, very bad man," Gibbs informed, helping her from the car by her thin, pale arm. He practically carried her to the bottom step, so she wouldn't slip.

"I can walk alone, you know," she said, turning to him after unlocking her door.

"I was using you to brace myself."

"Sure you were. Thanks, in advance, for your help."

"Don't know how much I'll provide. Good night, Ms. Chevalier."

"Leontine."

"Good night, Leontine."

Abruptly and unexpectedly, she leaned forward to kiss his snow-speckled cheek, then skipped lightly over the threshold and shut the door.

Phase One was hers.

Connor's ride home was melancholy. Once there, he fed Oreo (the cat), then himself almost as an afterthought. He washed the dishes (except Oreo's), and read until midnight, when the words began to merge. He fell asleep in his big leather chair and in the morning had a crick in his neck and the taste of disquietude on his tongue.

Dreams.

Chapter 4

"How about you come take me to the store for provisions, then I'll fix supper here?" Leontine Chevalier's voice came through the speaker phone as Gibbs did the last of a hundred push-ups. Through his den window, the weak solstice sun cast a dull glow upon his naked back as he pistoned.

"But I envisioned homemade biscuits, mounds of mashed potatoes, a slab of ham—"

"My hair's a mess," she interrupted. "Besides, I don't feel like mashed potatoes."

"And you don't look like mashed potatoes." Gibbs rolled onto his back for two hundred crunches. "Okay. Give me an hour."

"Make it an hour and a half," she said, and hung up.

Inside, the mobile home was neat and clean and orderly. And very small. Nestled in the westernmost corner of a low-rent park (complete with snow-dusted cars up on blocks, a weedy playground boasting a swing set with no swings, and a half dozen leafless trees here and there), its exterior was faded green, and its storm door was bereft of glass. A faded-blue Pacer squatted in the front yard; although not up on blocks, it was anyone's guess whether it ran. Perhaps this was the car that was "on the fritz."

Leontine Chevalier set her grocery bag—paper, not plastic—on a faded-rose chair near the door and called softly, "Marlene?" The doorway at the far end of the hall emitted a lean, pale, dark-haired girl of eighteen or so, obviously groggy from an interrupted nap. Connor Gibbs set his duffle at his feet and absorbed the surroundings: couch by a double window, opposite the front door where he stood; wooden granny rocker just this side of the hallway down which Marlene was approaching from his left; open kitchen area to his immediate right, dominated by a glass-topped table and three mismatched chairs, a faded-red refrigerator, and a nearly new stove. No microwave, no stack of cookbooks, no knife rack; one mottled toaster, no crumbs in sight. Everything was spotless, in its place, and on its last legs, except for the stove. Prosperity did not dwell here.

"Connor Gibbs," Leontine was saying, "this is Marlene Barefoot, my babysitter when I can afford her."

Connor turned his head toward the girl and offered a smile, not returned, whether from unfriendliness or indifference he couldn't determine. No matter. He wasn't running for office.

"Jared's been down about an hour," Marlene reported, knuckling one eye and yawning hippo-like. (No wisdom teeth.) "Took most of a bottle, so he didn't fret much, just went right to sleep."

"That's good," Leontine said, passing to the teenager a meager wad of currency, which Marlene pocketed. Then she brushed past Connor and departed.

"Bye," Leontine said to the teen, retrieving her groceries and heading for the fridge. "Sorry about Marlene. Kids these days aren't much on manners."

Shrugging, Connor said, "Were they ever?"

"Yes, in my daddy's house. He'd've back-handed me if I treated an adult that way."

Gibbs dismissed the subject with a wave of his hand. "Forget it."

"Let me stick this stuff in the cold, and I'll show you around the manse."

The refrigerator opened and closed, then down the hall they went, stopping at the first door—a tiny room with a single bed, a chair, one inexpensive floor lamp, a poster of Michael Jordan on the wall beside the bed, well-used tennis shoes beside a sliding closet door, half a basketball peeping out from under the bed.

"Eddie's room."

"Where's Eddie?" asked Gibbs.

"At my sister-in-law's, in New Jersey." Leontine moved down the hall to the second room, which contained an army cot, rolled sleeping bag, a folding beach chair unsturdily made of aluminum and cotton fabric, an upended milk crate atop which rested a table lamp with no shade, its bulb and base showing not a trace of dust.

"This'll be your room. Hope it's all right," she said.

"It's fine." He piled his plunder on the floor at the foot of the cot.

"Bathroom's right there," she said, retreating into the hall and pointing to a third door. He glanced inside. Faded purple shower curtain, mildew-free; two clean and folded towels on a rack over the gleaming toilet; various toiletry items on the counter beside the sink, everything strategically placed according to frequency of use. He looked behind the door: pale yellow washing machine; no space for a dryer.

Stepping through the last doorway, Leontine said quietly, "This is my room. Jared sleeps in here with me." There was a double bed, and a built-in dresser between two closets. On the other side of the bed, next to the dresser, was a crib; inside the crib, covered with a faded sky-blue blanket, slept four-month-old Jared, full of formula and resting peacefully, despite no father.

And recently, almost no brother.

Connor tiptoed over to the crib and looked down, his face a kaleidoscope of emotions, then turned away abruptly. A bit too abruptly for Leontine. *Wonder why,* she thought, and went to prepare supper while Connor phoned Blister, then rummaged through his suitcase, preparing to stay.

"I'll do that," she objected as he ran water into the kitchen sink.

"You cooked."

"I know, but—"

"I'll do my share. When you cook, I scrub."

She relented. "Okay, but only if we swap off and you do some of the cooking. I'm pretty slack in that department."

"The food was fine," he disagreed, dipping a dish into sudsy water.

"Right. Scrambled eggs and livermush. Am I a chef or what?"

A smile from the dishwasher. "And toast. Don't forget the toast."

"A bit overdone, you neglected to mention."

"Toaster's set too high. Not your fault."

She chuckled. "What a husband you'd make."

His response was to let the conversation dry up.

"Ever been one?" she pressed.

"I'm not here to answer personal questions. I'm here to keep you from shooting someone. By the way, where's the gun you used on those dogs?"

"The police took it when they slapped me in irons."

"How were you planning to murder Mr. Helms? With a chainsaw?"

"Good idea, but no, I've got another gun."

He set a cup on the drainboard. "Get it."

She didn't move. He looked at her over his shoulder. "Was I ambiguous?"

"I'm not used to being told what to do."

"You came to me for help, not the other way around," he replied, rinsing a handful of flatware.

"I know."

"Then go get the gun. And get used to doing what I tell you, at least so far as your immediate situation is concerned."

She disappeared into the master bedroom for fifteen seconds, came back carrying a shotgun as long as a vaulting pole and held it out to him.

"My hands are wet," he said. "Is it loaded?"

"Well, as Big Sam used to say, an unloaded gun isn't worth a tinker's durn. Big Sam never used foul language."

"Can you unload it without blowing a hole in something?"

Grim smile. "I only know one way to unload it. Pull the trigger five times."

"In that case, lay it on the floor, muzzle toward the wall. I'll get to it in a minute."

She carefully put down the shotgun, bending at the knees, then straightened and said with more than a touch of coy, "Since you seem to have the kitchen duties well in hand, I'm going to take a shower and wash my hair. Think you can restrain your masculine impulses while I do so?"

"I'll try. If not, I've a pound of saltpeter in my duffle for emergency use. Keep it as antidote to the rhino horn."

Once again her throaty chuckle. "Salt what?"

"Go take your bath."

Light of step as she went down the hall; Phase Two seemed to be falling neatly into place.

Connor could hear the shower running full tilt when Jared woke in full cry, so he dried his hands on a dish towel, traversed the hall, and scooped up the child, whose protests did not cease. One sniff told the story. Gibbs found diapers and wipes in a dresser drawer, along with a vinyl mat to receive the baby. Spreading the mat on the bed, he deposited the fretful child on its back, removed the two safety pins, unfolded the redolent cloth carefully, so nothing would escape, noted with relief the relatively solid stool, removed the diaper with its contents safely inside and stashed it out of the baby's reach, wiped the child's bottom free of residue, put the soiled wipe atop the diaper, noticed some redness and searched for a can of powder, found none, so used another wipe to moisten and soothe the afflicted area, gently grasped tiny flailing legs at the ankles to lift the buttocks free of the mat and slip a clean diaper underneath. In a jiffy, everything was snug and pinned in place. The child ceased fussing, to observe closely the unfamiliar giant attending his needs.

"There you go, big guy," Connor said in a calm voice, lifting Jared to his left shoulder and holding him there with one big palm on the seat of his diaper. The baby squirmed a bit, but otherwise seemed reasonably content. Suspecting that the child, while not actually hungry, might nonetheless be feeling an urge to suckle, Gibbs moved back to the kitchen, found sterile bottles in a cupboard, filled one with lukewarm tap water, reversed the nipple on the cap, screwed it down tight, and offered it to Jared, who immediately snared the nipple like a vacuum, his small cheeks working. In a moment, eyes closed, his frantic suction lessened in intensity and settled into a sustainable rhythm. Connor sat in the rocker, cradled the contented baby on his left forearm, and rocked.

By the time the lady of the house reappeared—engulfed in a robe two sizes too large and with her hair wrapped in a towel—the baby was sound asleep. Connor, rocking back and forth, his own eyes shut, breathed as slowly and regularly as the child. The forgotten bottle lay against his broad chest. Leontine shook her head at this unexpected scene, then sat on the sofa and watched the pair for a long time.

Before going to bed herself, she gently took Jared from Connor's arms, laid the boy back in his crib, placed the shotgun under the couch out of sight, and switched off the lights.

Early the next morning, snowed in but toasty, Leontine Chevalier watched as Connor unloaded her shotgun, his movements quick, deft, economical, his familiarity and confidence with firearms evident. "You're used to guns," she commented.

He nodded.

"You like them?"

He shrugged.

"What's to like, right? They're just tools," she answered for him. "That's what Big Sam used to say."

He nodded again, placing five red-and-brass-colored shells back in their original box.

"Aren't you the chatterbox?" she chided.

"I'm not much interested in the subject."

"In your line of work, I'd think you'd carry a gun all the time."

He shook his head.

"You don't have one?"

"I didn't say that. I just don't often carry one."

"Why not?"

He took the shotgun back to his room and placed it under the cot. The shells went on a shelf high in the closet, behind a stack of children's books. Having followed him to the doorway, she asked again, "Why don't you carry a gun?"

He shrugged.

"I really want to know."

"What difference does it make?"

"Well, you're my bodyguard, sort of. I'm entitled to know how you feel about things like guns."

"I thought I was protecting someone from you."

She turned away in disgust, returning to the sofa. He joined her in the living room, taking the rocker.

"I'm pretty big," he said.

"I've noticed. So?"

"So most men don't press me. I guess my size deters them, and that's fine. Whatever I once felt I had to prove, I did long ago." He paused, his face mysteriously clouded, then continued. "When push comes to shove, I usually manage to take care of myself without weapons, or firearms at any rate. If a situation warrants, I utilize what's at hand. A rolled-up newspaper, or a broomstick. A set of keys. Improvisation."

"But you're obviously familiar with guns. You must have used them, if only for target practice. I just wonder why you don't carry one," she said.

For a while, he was silent. Then he said, "I don't like having a gun within easy reach except under very unusual circumstances."

"You haven't told me why."

"And I don't intend to."

"Fine," she said—unhappy with the fruit of this conversation—and went to check on the baby.

What he could have told her was that in the past he'd often used guns. Against men. But whenever he did, those around him tended to die in wholesale lots.

Chapter 5

I HATE THE FUCKING CRAWL, HE THOUGHT, SPUT-
tering and spitting. *Always get water in my fucking mouth,
and it tastes like shit. Too much fucking chlorine.* He made
it to the side of the pool and, having completed ten laps,
beached himself like a sperm whale.

"Whyn't you get a ladder put in?"

"Didn't need no fucking ladder when I was growing up,"
commented Gantt Helms.

"You ain't growing up no more, and you weigh as much
as a truckload of olives. Makes me sick to watch you drag
your lard ass up over the side. Oughta have a sign on it saying 'Wide Load.' What'd Pop say could he see you?"

"He can't, so shut the fuck up." Gantt Helms sank into a
deck chair, hairless pallid chest heaving from exertion. He
took several deep cleansing breaths, then coughed for thirty
seconds.

"Look at you," said brother Sherman, five-feet-nine and
140 pounds. "You look like Jabba the Hutt." He shook his
head sadly.

"I took after Ma. You're the one built like Pop, all skin
and bone."

"Don't forget pecker," Sherm admonished. "Hey, you took after Ma *there,* too."

"I said shut the fuck up."

"Yeah, I heard you. You hear me doing it, don't you."

Gantt took a pull from the Bud sitting poolside in a puddle of condensation. "Ugh! Tastes like warm piss!"

"*All* beer tastes like warm piss. In fact, I think it is. That's what you get for drinking at seven in the morning. I'd hate to see your liver."

"You won't. I'm an organ donor. It'll wind up in some fucking movie star. What time we got to be in court?"

"Lawyer said nine sharp."

"Fucking criminal negligence! My fucking dogs didn't *eat* that kid."

"They'll say you should've kept them locked up better."

"I can help it they dug under the fucking fence?"

"They'll say you should've sunk chicken wire three or four feet into the ground. Maybe electrified the fence."

"Yeah, and they can fucking pay for it, too!" Gantt threw the tepid Bud into the pool angrily, then crossed his arms over his breasts, his preferred pouting position. "Bitch shot two of my best dogs. They oughta arrest her."

"Uh, they did, brother."

Gantt seemed not to hear. "She'll pay one way or the other. Screw the law," he muttered.

Sherman didn't like hearing that. His younger sibling frequently displayed a proclivity for stupid moves, and going after this trailer-park bimbo would definitely be a lulu. No need trying to dissuade him now, though. Not in this mood. Time for a subject change. "When're the cars due in from Atlanta?"

"Late this afternoon."

"How many BMWs?"

"Two, why?"

"Bernie wants all you can—"

"*Fuck* Bernie! Let Chicago steal their own cars. This

batch is heading west. Bernie don't pay top dollar like the west coast crowd, and they never ask questions. Besides, Bernie's got a nose like fucking Pinocchio, and he's always poking it where it don't belong."

That was certainly true. "How's the weed situation up at Jefferson?"

"Little Boy's harvesting three plots this week," answered Gantt, getting to his flat, scabby feet. There was a boil on one great toe, and it hurt like hell. "Five more laps, then fuck it. And I don't give a shit what the doctor says." The splash he made diving was impressive. *Fuck the crawl,* he thought as he entered the water. *I'm breast-stroking these babies.*

And so he did, while his older brother finished a raisin bagel and called their bookie.

Chapter 6

THE NIGHT HAD DUMPED FOUR INCHES ON THE trailer park, and no one was moving except Mr. Gnack down the road. "There's Nicholas," Leontine pointed out, coffee cup to her lips. "He's from Maine originally. Old Nick loves to shovel snow." She took a heated sip.

"So tell me about Eddie," prompted Connor.

Leontine took another sip and turned away from the window. "Right after I shot his dogs, I called Gantt Helms on the phone. Told him his turn was next. Said that first I was going after his money, for my boys, then I was going to tack his raggedy hide to the side of a tobacco barn where it belonged."

"You really didn't, right?"

"I really *did*, and he didn't like it much."

"How could you tell?" said Connor, grinning.

"I'm sensitive that way. Maybe it was all the cursing and the threats and the way he kept banging the phone against something hard."

"Gantt's a subtle man."

She sat in the faded rose chair by the door. "So after a day or two, Eddie went back to school. That afternoon, when he was walking to his bus, he noticed two guys in a Caddy, just sitting and watching."

"On school grounds?"

"No, across the tracks on the west side."

"But they made no move? Didn't climb out, look threatening or anything?"

She shook her head while taking a sip, the steam rising around her thin face. "So I called Helms again, asked did he send two ugly dudes to spy on my boy."

"And his response?"

"He said he sure as hell did. So I asked why, and he laughed at me, then he said that what his dogs didn't finish, his goons would."

"Gantt's a class act."

She nodded and sipped. "But it scared me, for Eddie. So I trundled him off to Westampton, New Jersey, and my sister-in-law LouAnne. Make no mistake, Mr. Gibbs. I believed that man when he said he was gonna kill my boy. I still do."

Connor thought about it. Knowing Helms, she was probably right. "So Eddie's safe."

"As safe as I can make him, unless I pack him off to my cousin in Idaho. Or knock Helms over."

"Put that on the back burner for now." Gibbs looked at his watch. "Well, about time for your date with the judge. Leave me change into more appropriate garb." And he quit the room.

"Now don't we look sharp?" Leontine assessed as Connor came down the hall ten minutes later, resplendent in a Brooks Brothers charcoal two-piece, blue-and-white striped Gitman with a curved-spread collar, Robert Talbott tie, and polished Balli cap-toe lace-ups.

His smile was slightly awkward, as if he'd been caught doing one-arm pushups for a cluster of Dallas cheerleaders. "I figured it wouldn't hurt to dazzle the judge with sartorial splendor."

"Sartorial? You don't talk like a guy who's as big as the Chrysler Building."

"And you don't dress like an unemployed lady who lives in a mobile home park," he said, returning the left-handed compliment and immediately regretting it when her face fell.

Her face may have fallen, but the knowing eyes were not downcast. "I'll have you know, sir, that I spent a good portion of Big Sam's burial insurance on this outfit, for the funeral."

"I just meant—" he started.

"I know what you meant," she said, and reached out to pat his muscular shoulder. "Some day, you'll learn to keep that size twelve out of your mouth."

"You reckon?" He held a hand out toward the door.

"Then again . . ." she replied, taking a deep breath and grabbing her purse. "Okay. Let's get it over with."

Chapter 7

LITTLE BOY NEEDED TO MOVE THE CHARGER'S engine block from one place on the oil-stained concrete garage floor to another, but the hoist was in use. Well, not actually in use; Yip had jerked the V-6 out of the Pontiac, then left the motor dangling. Hell, why not? It *was* noon wasn't it? Little Boy looked down at the big 440 Magnum block on the floor, of cast iron and heavy as . . . well, an engine block. He bent his bulk—all six-feet-five inches and 285 pounds of it—to the task, lifting with his legs more than his back, at least until he straightened. Staggering the twenty-odd feet to his workbench, he deposited the awkward hunk of metal atop it—CLUNK!—heaved a sigh and looked at his hand. Pooh, he'd torn a nail, to the quick. It hurt, too. He sucked on it, kicked a socket wrench under the bench, and strode out the open bay door.

Falling snow greeted him. *Feel like I'm in one of those glass balls with the penguins inside, or Santa Claus,* he thought as he walked. Barbecue Heaven was less than a quarter-mile, due south as Little Boy tracked up the snow. Everyone else had driven, so his were the only footprints in the field. A starling pecked at something nearby, its reward meager. Crows swooped, intent on theft. The starling, out-numbered, fluttered away. Little Boy stooped to retrieve a fallen feather freshly shed, its barbules separated. He smoothed them into a barb, marveling as always at how they attached themselves zipperlike; keratin was amazing stuff, the base protein of hair and nails and horns and scales. And feathers. He tickled his lips with this one as he paced, bringing goosebumps. *Pretty cold, should have worn a coat,* he thought as he approached the restaurant, stepped up onto its porch, opened and entered and crossed the warm room full of raucous diners masticating and palavering. Yip Stevens, too, over by the wood-burning stove, a load of slaw bound for his mouth, nodding his leonine head at something someone said, unaware of Little Boy until it was too late. The slaw stopped en route. Little Boy, too, to stand glaring.

"What?" said Yip, sallow and scared, and then he remembered. "Hey, I forgot to lower the Pony's engine," he pleaded, throat working, the smell of his fear in the room.

Little Boy said nothing.

Oh shit! everybody thought.

"I'm sorry, man," said Yip. "I'll run right back soon's I finish lunch and lift 'er down."

More nothing from Little Boy.

Yip's spoonful of slaw sank back to the plate. "Maybe I should run do it now," he suggested.

Little Boy just stared.

"Yeah, that's what I'll do, then come back and finish my grub," Yip exclaimed, and jumped out of his chair, skirted carefully his implacable antagonist, and skittered across the silent room like a leaf in the wind.

Little Boy ate the slaw.

Chapter 8

THE SHORT STOCKY DETECTIVE PLOPPED WEARILY onto the bench beside a uniformed co-worker, both of them outside Courtroom A waiting to testify. "How you hanging, Bart?"

The uniformed cop, a swarthy man of Hungarian descent, dipped his chin in greeting. "I hope they nail Helms. My little girl's the same age as the Chevalier kid. Could've happened to her just as easy."

The stocky plainclothes skimmed a hand across his face, paused, thumb and forefinger pinching his nose. Speaking through the fingers, he said, "Naw. She don't live in no trailer park."

At the far end of the hall a tall thick man rounded the corner, accompanied by a pale slender woman in funeral raiment. Plainclothes pointed with one of his chins, and the uniform swung his head to look. "Seems pretty cocky for someone up on two charges, don't she?" commented the corpulent cop.

"Who's the big fashion plate?"

"Name's Gibbs," answered the plainclothes, massaging his oily round face and thinking, *I shoulda shaved this morning.*

"What's he to her?" asked the uniform.

Plainclothes shrugged, straightened his tie (a brightly hued Rush Limbaugh "No Boundaries" number his conservative father-in-law had afflicted him with for Christmas), and said, "How do I know? Bodyguard maybe. I hear she threatened Helms."

"That the big bastard's line? Security?"

"Among other things," mumbled the plainclothes, climbing to his feet. "Excuse me while I go splash my boots. Save this spot." He ambled off to the john while his pal gazed surreptitiously at Connor Gibbs and wondered what the fat detective had meant by "other things."

Gibbs steered his charge toward the bench and seated her next to the uniform. "That place is taken," said the cop.

Without so much as a glance, Gibbs said, "It sure is."

The uniform let it go.

Leontine's court appearance went better than expected. The district attorney considered the circumstances leading up to her shooting of the rottweilers—and the fact that she'd had no previous brushes with the law—and agreed to drop the charges. An SPCA representative present in the courtroom nearly had apoplexy, but swallowed his objections after a brief, private, eye-to-eye discussion with Connor Gibbs, *sotto voce*. The man left immediately following the conference, his balding crown as red as a radish.

"What'd you say to him?" asked Holmes Crenshaw as the pair escorted Ms. Chevalier from the courtroom.

"Told him I'd buy him a new red wagon if he wouldn't push this thing. He promised not to."

Holmes chuckled. "What'd you really say?"

"I appealed to his higher instinct."

"Which one?"

"Survival."

Holmes laughed out loud.

"You threatened him?" Leontine said.

"He seemed to think so. Regardless, he's gone."

Leontine, first through the double doors leading from the courtroom, stopped in the hall, turned, offered a hand to Crenshaw. "I want to thank you for everything."

"No prob," he said, patting her delicate mitt. "Well, I'll leave you to Connor. My next case is coming up." Back into the courtroom he went.

"Ready to go?" from Gibbs.

"Not by a long shot. I want to see what they do to Helms," Leontine responded.

"Why?"

"If they do their job, then maybe I won't have to kill him after all."

"Criminal negligence isn't much of a crime, and tough to prove. If they do convict, it'll bring a slap on the wrist and a small fine. Better for you to seek retribution through a civil suit and not dwell on the criminal aspects. Most likely he'll walk."

She went over to an empty bench and sat. "Can you get me some coffee? I need a caffeine hit, bad."

He dug into a pocket for change, counted what he found, ordered, "You stay right there," and hoofed it out of sight around a corner. Two minutes later, Gantt Helms came down the corridor, accompanied by his lawyer and his brother Sherm. They paused not ten feet away. No one paid her any attention.

"I can't fucking believe this," Gantt was saying. "Ten thousand dollars bond!"

"Watch your language," Sherman hissed, dipping his pate toward the woman.

Gantt glanced Leontine's way, then dismissed her as of no consequence. "She's prob'ly heard worse. Being outside criminal court, she ain't no fucking nun."

"Even so—" said the lawyer.

"Shut your fucking yap, Early. You don't tell me how to talk."

Early shut his yap.

Helms was in a stew. He perambulated in an ever widening circle, snuffing loudly through his nose every few seconds; he had allergies and was dripping relentlessly. Once, he started to wipe with the sleeve of his jacket, but Sherman stopped him: "Whoa, brother. That suit's navy. The smear'll show."

That made Gantt even madder, realizing that he should have worn beige or avocado. Sherm handed him a tissue, which took care of the drip but not the foul mood. "I still can't believe all this shit," Gantt complained. "And all over some fucking kid who shouldn't even have—"

He stopped speaking due to a sudden, piercing, unbearable pain caused by a very hard, sharp heel, which the woman had brought down with great force onto his foot, the point of the heel impacting—like a surgical strike—precisely on his inflamed boil. He wanted to scream, to blaspheme, to shout "FUCK!" at least twice, but the pain was too intense, too incredibly *disabling*, like a quick knee to the groin. All he could do was hold his breath, lean on the wall, and try not to lose breakfast.

Sherm reached out to grab the woman, but his attention was diverted by molten liquid running down the back of his collar. It burned its way down his neck, his spine, and on into his nether regions as he hopped from foot to foot, arms flailing, shouting "Ah, ah, ah, ah!"

"Sorry," said Connor Gibbs, the epitome of concern. "Did I spill coffee on you? Here." He offered a napkin.

Over by the wall, brother Gantt found voice, wailing like a gelded banshee, which drew from the courtroom a pair of deputies, their mouths agape in disbelief at the unseemly disruption.

"Quiet, sir!" shushed the larger of the pair, his directive aimed at Gantt. "You, too!" from his counterpart, speaking to Sherman, still engaged in his lobster dance. Then the bigger one asked, "What happened out here?"

Gantt Helms—his overstuffed backside propped against the wall, one shod foot on the tile floor, the other (recently unshod) held protectively in a pudgy hand, his leg crossed at the knee—pointed angrily at the slim woman seated demurely across the hall. "That bitch stomped my foot!" he squalled.

The deputies stared at the innocuous lady.

"And he," yelled Sherman, his pain-induced jig finally winding down, "poured something hot all over me!"

The deputies stared at Connor Gibbs, standing quietly twenty feet away with nothing in his hands. Turning to Early, the attorney (seated now beside the woman to remove himself from the loop), the smaller deputy said, "You see any of this?"

"Not a thing. I was reviewing a case." He tapped his attaché with a forefinger.

The deputies exchanged looks. The larger one (whose name was Jim) said to his partner (whose name was also Jim): "Got clowns on our hands," then looked hard at the brothers Helm. "You boys keep it down, hear?" he instructed.

"Yeah, any more noise, and we'll show you the street," underscored the smaller Jim.

"Well, fuck!" exclaimed Gantt Helms in disbelief.

"And watch your mouth. There's a lady present," warned Jim the Smaller, then shouldered through the swinging doors. Big Jim tossed the Helms faction a final withering look and followed suit.

In the mini-van, on the way home, Leontine broke the silence. "How'd you get rid of the coffee cup so fast?"

"Flattened it and stuck it in my pocket."

She smiled slightly, then leaned her head against the door and dozed off.

Chapter 9

SHE RAISED HER HEAD. "WHERE ARE WE?"

"My house."

"Nice house. Whose convertible is that?" she asked, squinting and still half asleep.

"Mine," Connor said.

"You a ragtop man?"

"When it's not snowing." He levered his big frame out of the Sienna.

She yawned, her pale hand hovering politely in front of her mouth. "No offense. I just didn't picture you . . ."

He leaned back inside. "As a convertible buff?"

"Well, you're so . . . tall."

"I cut a hole in the roof when I drive with the top up," he quipped, and departed for his stoop.

"Sure, I'll come right in," Leontine mumbled to herself, pivoting out of her seat. *He has Christmas decorations up here, too, and it's only the fifth. What bachelor does that?* she thought, as her long legs carried her to the doorway.

Connor poked his head around the jamb and said, "Come in. Have a seat. I put on coffee for you since Sherman Helms took a bath in yours."

Awash with gratitude, Leontine said, "You're a life saver." A white cat, smallish and thin, sashayed into the living room and sprang onto Leontine's lap, adjusted its lithe body this way and that, then settled cloudlike dead center. Leontine rubbed the small head, drawing a felicitous purr.

"Careful, Oreo's a bit treacherous," Gibbs warned from the kitchen doorway. "When she doesn't want to be rubbed, she generally lets you know by biting. Without warning. The only person she never bites is me."

"'Cause you beat her?"

"Unmercifully," he agreed, bringing coffee in a steaming cup—no saucer—and presenting it with a flourish. "I'll brook no blame for what that stuff does to your body." He stroked the cat lightly before leaving.

In five minutes, he was back, having divested himself of his morning finery in favor of tan Dockers and a black knit shirt. "You ready to go?" he queried.

"Aren't you going to show me around?"

"I just came by to feed the animals."

"Animals plural?"

"There's Oreo and my two piranhas."

"Wow. Can I see them?"

"I'd rather not. They're uneasy with strangers. Puts them off their feed."

"What do you feed them?"

"Strangers."

Leontine laughed, then said, "One refill first?" and held out her cup.

Connor brought the coffeepot, refilled the hollow ware, instructed, "Yell when you're ready," stroked the cat once more—against the grain, causing the furry tail to flop twice in mild irritation—and repaired to the kitchen.

"Why on earth did you name her Oreo? She's white as a winter ermine."

No answer.

"Connor? Did you hear me?"

"I heard you."

"Well?"

Still no answer.

"I guess you don't want to say."

"I guess."

"Why not?"

No answer. So she drank her coffee and mused.

"I loved the Christmas decorations. Did you put them up?" Leontine commented when again in the van, no longer sleepy now that she was suffused with caffeine.

"All by myself," answered Connor Gibbs.

"Unusual to see a man who lives all alone go to that much trouble for Christmas."

Only traveling sounds in response: muted growl from the engine, the whir of all-weather radials, spray of melted snow as they splashed along. Reflections of pale sunlight pooled on her irises as Leontine gazed out the window, thinking, inhaling the dense wintry smells.

"How'd you choose the name Oreo?" she segued neatly.

No response, just feigned concentration on driving.

"I like this van." She withdrew briefly. "Plenty of headroom, even for someone your size."

Nod of agreement.

"How'd you pick Oreo for the cat's name?"

No response.

Pressing the issue: "Why won't you tell—"

"When we moved into the house, the neighbors on one side—long since moved away—owned a short-haired cat, solid black. Part Maine coon, I believe. Our neighbor on the other side—still there—had a mixed Persian. Also black." He glanced at her with *Now figure it out* in his eyes.

"Oreo was the white center."

Perfunctory smile, on and off like a firefly.

"Who's we?"

"Beg pardon?"

"You said *we* moved in."

No further comment.

"Who named the cat?"

But that was all Connor had to say on the subject.

Jared was cooing and drooling onto Connor's shirt, stubby little legs kicking happily, as Connor lay on his back in the living room with Jared belly-down against his broad chest.

"He might ruin that shirt," said Leontine from the hallway, a stack of folded diapers in her arms.

"Drool never ruined a shirt, not in my experience. Even if it did, it'd be worth it, he's having so much fun. And I have other shirts."

She shook her head. "I never met a man like you."

Connor cooed back at Jared, delighting the baby and inducing him to kick harder.

"Good thing you're so tall," she observed. "If you weren't, or he was a little longer, he'd kick you right in the balls."

"Don't I know it. It's why I have his head waaay up here under my chin."

As Jared emitted a particularly fulsome dollop of saliva, shirtward bound, a knock sounded at the door. Leontine opened it, spoke quietly to someone female for a moment, then turned to Connor. "It's a reporter from Channel 2."

"Yeah?"

"She wants to interview me."

"Jared too?"

"I don't think so."

He nuzzled Jared's headful of curls with his chin. "Sounds like age discrimination. What do you think, little pal?"

"Excuse me?" Leontine pressed.

"Yes?"

"Should I talk to her?"

"Why not? Maybe get to watch yourself on the evening news."

"What do you think she wants from me?"

Connor looked up. "She'll probably mention Eddie, fish for some detail overlooked by the papers. Maybe want to know how you feel about the DA dropping the charges against you. That kind of human-interest pap."

"So it's all right if I talk to her?"

"I think so. Just don't let her bait you."

"Shouldn't you be there?"

"She's not interested in me, charming and sophisticated though I am. You'll be okay," he assured.

It was his worst decision in years, maybe ever. Its repercussions disrupted many lives.

And without doubt cost some.

Chapter 10

LITTLE BOY WAS AN INTERESTING AMALGAM, ONE part Welsh, one part Pima, one part Azerbaijani, one part Bulgarian, one part Peruvian, one part Norwegian, one part Thai, and one part Congolese. Slide Websen called him "that friggin' octoroon," but not to his face. No one knew Little Boy's full name—or even if he had a full name; everyone simply referred to him as Little Boy, except for Johnny Applewhite, the storekeep's adopted son, age six. Johnny called him Mr. Boy, as he was doing now: "Mr. Boy?" he said.

"Yes, Mr. Applewhite," said Little Boy, turning from his work.

"That Websen man wants you," from Johnny.

"He knows where to find me."

"He gimme a quarter to hunt you up."

"You did. Now go tell him where you found me."

"He'll be mad, like as not."

"He'll get over it, but be sure you get the quarter before you tell him."

"He give it to me 'fore I come, else I wouldn't have."

"Smart kid. I always say that when somebody asks. I tell 'em, 'That Johnny Applewhite, he's one smart kid.'"

Johnny beamed.

"You run along and give Slide my message. And mind you don't jump in any snow puddles."

Johnny looked down at his shoes. "Heck no, it'd roon my new tennies. My uncle'd whip me sound." The boy turned to go. "'Sides," he added, "it'd make my feets cold."

Off he squirted, jumping into four puddles on his way back to the store.

His uncle whipped him good.

"Gantt's sending up a pair of Majorcan Presas," Slide allowed.

Little Boy put down the cordless screwdriver and picked up a digital voltmeter.

"Wants Pepper to train them," Slide informed.

Little Boy put down the voltmeter and picked up an output transistor. "Pepper" was Pepperoy Jenesais-Quoi, a French-Canadian dog handler Little Boy knew.

"Dogs'll be here tomorrow," Slide enlightened.

Little Boy mounted the transistor and picked up a soldering iron.

"Any of this getting through to you?" Slide asked.

Little Boy picked up a second output transistor, mounted it, and soldered. Then he said, "Next time you send Johnny to find me, pay him a dollar. Can't buy anything for a quarter."

Websen played his tongue across a rough tooth. "Well, I told you. You don't get in touch with Pepper, it's your ass in a sling, not mine."

Little Boy finished soldering, put down the iron, plugged in the Onkyo receiver. The automatic tuner kicked in, and abruptly Anne Murray belted out "We Three Kings."

Loudly.

"Screw that noise," Slide said, and reached for the knob.

Little Boy's eyes cut to the reaching hand; the hand

stopped inches short of its goal. Little Boy's eyes shifted to Slide's; the hand quickly withdrew.

"You been told," Slide said curtly, then left.

Anne Murray sang on. Little Boy accompanied her. He liked Christmas music.

The small face was red, tear-stained. "Yes, Mr. Boy?"

Little Boy looked down. Johnny had his rubbers on. "You find a puddle?"

Unhappy nod.

"Your uncle whip you sound?"

Nod.

Little Boy gently pulled the child's collar aside to peer down his back. Welts. From a belt. "Can you find Pepper for me?" Little Boy said.

Johnny nodded, and not from disrespect; if he had tried to speak just then, his voice would have quavered. Very unmanly, especially in front of Mr. Boy, the ultimate man in Johnny's book.

"I'll give you five dollars," offered Little Boy.

Johnny shook his small head in refusal.

"Oh, you'll do it as a favor, right?"

Nod.

"All right. But a favor for a favor. We'll settle on something later. Deal?"

Nod of concurrence as off Johnny went in search of Pepper.

Little Boy went to the store. Anson Applewhite was there, removing the bung from a fresh keg. "Want a brewsky?" he asked as Little Boy darkened the stoop.

Little Boy shook his head. "Need a plug, though. You know my brand."

Anson Applewhite went behind the counter to fetch the plug, and Little Boy handed him a fiver. Applewhite dipped into the cash register as Little Boy bit off a chew, then pocketed his change and started to turn away. Then, as if in afterthought, he said, "Johnny's had a tough life, hasn't he?"

"Dang right," Applewhite agreed, shaking his head in commiseration.

"Heard your brother was an alcoholic, died in a car wreck, and that the kid's mom was a hophead. The baby had to be detoxed when he was born, I understand."

Applewhite shook his head and *tsk-tsked* at the injustice of it all.

Little Boy gestured him closer, glancing to each side as if to ensure the privacy of this conversation. Applewhite lent an inquisitive ear.

"Did you ever jump in a puddle when you were a boy, get your good shoes wet?"

Applewhite laughed conspiratorially. "You bet."

"Thought so. No crime to it."

"Hell, no. I remember this one time—"

Applewhite halted mid-remembrance because a big hand had snagged his shirtfront. Little Boy, nearly nose to nose, said quietly, "Don't hit the boy again. Give him time out, hide the remote, make him sit in the corner. But don't hit him. Ever. Understand?"

Applewhite gulped and nodded.

"If you do, I'll come for you like Moses parting the sea."

Another gulp and nod.

"You believe it?"

Vehement nod.

"Good." Little Boy released the shirt, spat a gloppy stain onto the countertop, stepped back. "Clean that up," he said, and was gone.

Anson Applewhite stood immobile for three minutes, fighting down a panic attack. His wife had observed everything from across the room and said nothing, though inwardly she smiled.

Because she had belt marks, too.

Chapter 11

THE LEAD STORY THAT MORNING DEALT WITH A severe ice storm in a contiguous county: Ten thousand homes without electricity; two deaths; damage in the millions; Federal aid might be sought. But now the good news: The weekend's ACC basketball schedule wouldn't be disrupted.

Thank goodness.

Then suddenly on the screen was a familiar lean face—a bit haggard in the thin winter sunlight, which would aid in extracting sympathy from viewers. *Leontine would prefer empathy,* Connor reflected as he tested formula on the inside of his wrist, one eye on the television and the other on the pot of hot water in which he'd been heating Jared's supper. "Perfect," he reported. "If he wasn't hungry, I'd drink it myself."

His jocularity went unappreciated; Leontine, on the couch holding the baby, was intent on the TV.

"May I have Jared now?" Gibbs said. She handed him over. Up to the waiting mouth went the bottle; air bubbles rose immediately as the boy's stomach began to fill. Connor sat in the rocker—knees drawn together, child in his lap, its chin facing him so he could monitor the meal—and watched the interview.

Things went well until the end, when the anchor said: "I understand you've hired private security, Ms. Chevalier."

"Yes, Connor Gibbs."

"And he is with you twenty-four hours a day?"

"More or less."

"Have you received threats?"

"Mr. Gibbs isn't my bodyguard, exactly."

Oh, no, Connor thought, the bottle suddenly forgotten. Jared didn't mind; he continued to suck with purpose.

Puzzled, but with every hair stiffly in place, the anchor queried, "Why hire him if not for protection?"

Connor shut his eyes, as if doing so might stave off imminent disaster.

It didn't. Onscreen, Leontine answered, "I hired him to stop me from shooting Gantt Helms."

After a brief but profound silence, the anchor, flustered but realizing that some kind of coup had been scored, finished with, "Uh, back to you, Dick."

But Connor didn't see it; his eyes were still closed. He kept them that way for a moment, then mumbled, "Well, the fat's in the fire now," and quietly patted Jared's tiny back until rewarded by a healthy *urp* and a modicum of white fluid, absorbed by the diaper strategically placed on Connor's shoulder.

"I just told the truth," advanced Leontine.

Connor began to bounce Jared lightly, to encourage sleep. Nope. Jared had other business; Connor could feel the tiny body tense. Even across the room, the result was olfactorily obvious. Leontine said, "Here, let me take care of it."

Handing the child to its mother, Connor followed them down the hall. "You realize what this means?"

"No, what?" she asked, retrieving the changing mat and placing it on the bed, then Jared atop that.

"You threw down the gauntlet."

"Exactly how did I do that?"

"You came right out and said that without someone holding you back, you'd go gunning for Gantt."

She straightened up to look him in the eye. "So? Without you here, I might."

"But, my dear, Helms can't take this lying down. He's an egomaniacal, sadistic blob of guano. That interview will force him to take action of some kind, and PDQ, or he'll lose face among his peers. Besides, old Gantt enjoys having people hurt."

"You know him?"

"I know of him. And I know his kind. You just spat fighting words at a major underworld creep—at least major on the local level—and in front of a television audience. As of right now, you'll *need* a bodyguard." Gibbs paused dramatically, not for effect but because of a sudden chilling thought. He looked down at little Jared there on the bed, freshly diapered, powdered, content . . .

Vulnerable.

"Maybe so will he," said Gibbs.

And Connor was right. Soon the baby would indeed need a bodyguard. Desperately.

And get one.

By then it would be too late.

Chapter 12

"WHO'S WE?" LEONTINE HAD ASKED . . .

. . . *We* . . .

Connor Gibbs lay on his back on the undersized cot, thick fingers laced behind his head, staring up at the water-marked ceiling, hearing with his mind's ear, seeing with his mind's eye, a rending sorrow waiting beneath the surface calm, squidlike, for a chance to rise and grip his heart. Again. It was always thus when he lingered, remembering . . .

. . . *We.*

He'd been right there beside her when they lifted the baby free of her abdomen, holding his wife's hand and doing his best to keep her calm. She'd received only mild anaesthesia, so there was pain. Their newborn son was blue, which they'd covered in Lamaze, but insufficiently as preparation for the shocking reality. He couldn't let Felicia know (she was under enough stress at that moment), so he assured her everything was under control. She was fine; the child was fine. For two interminable minutes, he was scared speechless. Then his son had hollered, blessedly squalled, irate, informing the room: "I'M ALIVE! I CAN BREATHE!" Connor, swept with joy, turned to his wife and said, "See?" She answered, "It hurts." He told the doctor who immediately ordered the anaesthesiologist to put her under. Then Doc and Daddy took the baby—warmly wrapped but still voicing outrage at the miserable treatment—to another room, where a nurse handed Connor a bottle of fluid, saying, "Feed your son." He did.

And again and again over the years, countless times, through the transition from liquid to solids, spooning pureed prunes and similar unpalatable fare into his growing child, who played and crawled, walked and ran, learned to throw balls and socks and trucks and rocks, and once a cousin's hamster.

Felicia was Features Editor for a local newspaper during the day, working out of an office downtown, and aced college courses weekday nights. Weekends were spent with friends while Connor cared for their son. Gibbs quit the Agency with little warning, much to their irritation. They plied him with all manner of inducements, to no avail. Connor's reasoning was based on two absolutes: (1) if he went back to being a field operative, his new son had a good chance of losing a papa; (2) he had no desire to be away from his child for any length of time, especially with Felicia so seldom home.

The Agency—undeterred by his continued refusals and desperate to regain the use of his considerable talents (some inborn, some derived from extensive training)—resorted to blackmail. A mistake. Connor was not only big and strong and cunning and lethal, he was no fool. Squirreled away he had reams of incriminating missives, photographs, names, places, dates. Copies too, of everything, distributed among trusted colleagues from Panama to Sri Lanka. Should anything happen to Connor, or someone close to him, even something as innocuous as a fatal automobile accident, everyone to whom he had entrusted the aforementioned material would release same to various newspapers, both left- and right-oriented. The Agency quickly backed off, and each year since had sent a nice Christmas card and a fruitcake. Anonymously of course.

Connor coached soccer, T-ball, basketball, and badminton; his son Cameron engaged in them all. The boy was a natural athlete, strong and supple and possessed of the lightning reflexes acquired through his father's DNA. Between sports, Cameron's paternal grandfather taught him the violin; his maternal grandmother home-schooled the child, not only for the educational benefits of one on one, but to hold negative peer pressure to a minimum. Cameron's social life revolved around athletics, scouts, Sunday school, and play with selected neighborhood friends.

Then, after all those wonderful years during which time Gibbs and his son were virtually inseparable, Felicia Atcheson-Gibbs earned her final Master's degree. Rather than spending her now-abundant free time with her family, she elected to hobnob with an ever-widening pool of friends. The results for Connor and Cameron were devastating . . .

Gibbs sat up abruptly, the memories too harsh, too debilitating. He went to the kitchen for a cup of tea. Leontine heard him and started to get up to see what was wrong, but something told her not to. So she lay awake for an hour, until he had finished his tea, his pacing, his angst, and she heard the cot creakingly protest his weight once more. Then she drifted off . . .

To dream of rain on trees . . . unheeded pleas . . .

And death.

Chapter 13

"THE FUCKING CUNT! I WANT HER DEAD, HEAR me! *D-O-A!*" shouted Gantt Helms, pacing the room, a stogie clenched between yellowed teeth, his right forefinger stabbing the air for emphasis. He was miffed.

"Now, Mr. Helms," Manning interjected, "you've already got a criminal negligence charge to deal with, not to mention the still-pending lawsuit from that last incident. Something like this would just—"

"Fucking DEAD, you hear me! Dead! Dead! Dead! Raped and *then* dead! By fucking Little Boy, I hear he's hung like a horse! Then dragged behind that old flatbed truck until she's *nothing but raw fucking meat!* You hear me! *Raw fucking meat!*"

Sherman, trying to calm, said, "Now, brother—"

"Then burn the fucking bitch! Pour lighter fluid on her sorry ass and torch her! Make her scream! She needs someone to keep her from whacking *me*! I'll show her whack! Rape her and drag her and burn what's left! YOU FUCKING HEAR ME!" *Really* miffed, old Gantt.

"Mr. Helms, don't—"

Gantt grabbed Manning by the shirtfront, heaved him out

of his chair—a nicely padded wingback, basically mustard with brown flowers—and put his schnoz into the smaller man's face.

"Fucking dead, you hear me!"

Manning placed the muzzle of a snub-nosed .357 Magnum revolver against Helms' protuberant abdomen and said, "If you don't let go of me right now, I'm gonna blow your navel out through your asshole."

Manning meant it. Helms knew it. So, miffed but not suicidal, he let go the shirt.

"Never," warned Manning, "never touch me again. *Comprende?*"

Helms stared hard from piglike eyes, first at Manning, then at the revolver. Sherman said conciliatory, "He's upset, Harry. Cut him some slack."

"Yeah, fuck it," agreed Helms, turning away. "I'm just letting off steam. Sit down and drink your fucking eggnog." He crossed the huge room billowing smoke—courtesy of Cuba by way of Miami—and sank into a sofa.

Danny Manning straightened his tie, his shirt, then replaced the revolver in its holster, and resumed his seat. Soon a rime of warm eggnog decorated his philtrum.

"Clean off your fucking lip, you slob," ordered Gantt, then: "You two know I can't let that bitch get away with what she said."

"Why not?" asked brother Sherman.

"Why not! Because I can't, that's why not."

"Now there's a good reason."

"Don't start with me, Sherm! I ain't letting no woman say she needs someone to keep her from knocking me over!"

"You mean if she'd said she needed someone to help her pop you, that'd be okay?" laughed Sherman.

"At least it woulda been a *compliment*," accent on the final syllable. "Putting it like she did sounded like the skinny broad actually thinks she could bump me."

"So who cares, Helms?" from Manning, taking liberties

with protocol now that he'd gotten away with threatening his boss.

"Helms? *Helms*? What happened to *Mister* fucking Helms?"

"Gee, I'm sorry, *Mister* freakin' Helms."

"Harry?" said Sherman. "My brother takes this situation more seriously than you. And just because you stuck a gun in his gut and then sat down all apiece, that doesn't mean you can be disrespectful. See where I'm coming from?"

"Sure. Sorry, Mr. Helms." Though the words were properly contrite, the attitude was not. An irritant, but the Helms duo required Manning's special services from time to time, so they let it go.

Sherman to his sibling: "What's your plan?"

"Send a couple boys over to the trailer park, teach that bimbo some fucking manners."

"With Connor Gibbs around? That's crazy," Manning insisted.

"The hell it is. I hear he doesn't carry. Well, my guys do. One of 'em'll stick a piece in the big dickhead's ear while the other one crushes his fucking knees with a crowbar. Then they'll tend to the bitch."

"Who you gonna send?" asked Sherman.

"Mo and Iggy." When his brother started to object, Gantt held out a determined palm, warding it off. "I've heard the drift on Gibbs, same as you. I know he's bigger than the *Poseidon,* but he ain't crazy like Mo, or mean as hell like Iggy. Him and that skinny cunt'll wish they *were* dead!" he predicted, pounding his fat fist on a padded arm of the sofa and farting loudly. The room, despite its size, reeked of cigar smoke and flatulence. Sherman, though possessed of an unpleasant sense of foreboding, squelched his objections to Gantt's plan.

Most unfortunate.

Chapter 14

THE NEXT MORNING, CONNOR GIBBS—AFTER going home to feed Oreo and check his mail—had stopped at a video store to pick up a copy of *Miracle on 34th Street,* the recent version, with Richard Attenborough as Saint Nick. He also rented a VCR; Leontine had only an old, tired television set.

"This is great," she said now, sitting beside him on the couch with Jared cradled on her left arm, eager for sustenance. "I've never seen this one. Just the one with Natalie Wood, on TV lots of times when I was growing up. After Jared's finished, I'll fix us some popcorn."

As she directed a bottle to her son's eager mouth, Connor said, "I'll wait 'til he's finished to start it, so you won't miss any of the movie when you go to put him down."

A considerate man, she mused, *and handsome as all get out. He's probably in his mid-thirties, and is great with kids, so he's likely been married. Why would any woman let the likes of him get away? A drunk? Not the type, and dope certainly wouldn't appear to be his thing. And he obviously has money,* she concluded. *Let's go fishing and see what happens . . .*

"I considered breast-feeding Jared," she sighed coyly. "I wanted to, but . . ."

"But what?"

"He'd have starved." Slight downward tilt of the chin, tiny enigmatic smile.

He countered, "You're slim, but you're not flat-chested."

"How gallant."

"Just factual."

She laid her dark eyes upon him. "How do you know? I usually wear loose-fitting blouses."

"You fill those out nicely enough." He cleared his throat uneasily, despite having played this game before, which didn't make it easier unless you were a eunuch, and he wasn't.

"I never caught you staring."

"I don't have to stare to notice that you're a comely woman."

She laughed. "I've never heard that word used in conversation."

"Learned it from my dad. When I was a kid he would often say, 'Your mama's a comely lass.' I wasn't sure what it meant, but in third grade, I finally got around to looking it up. It made me happy that not only did he think that about Mom, but that he would tell me. One time, I mentioned it to her."

"What'd she say?"

"Nothing. Just smiled all the way down to her socks."

"That's sweet."

"Sure, but the value lay in the fact that they felt that way about each other."

A knock sounded at the door, barely audible. Connor cleared his throat again. *If he's too embarrassed to stand, I'll know I reached him.*

"You expecting anyone?" he asked.

"Nope. Sometimes Marlene will come by before a hot date, to borrow a pair of my jeans. Although I'm leaner than she is, she can squeeze into them if she lays down to put them on. But she usually calls before she comes over."

Obviously not embarrassed, Gibbs was already up and moving. He peered out the window by the door and saw nothing but dim light from the sixty-watt porch lamp. He went for the shotgun, quickly poked three shells into its tubular magazine, racked the bolt, set the safety, and returned to place it beside Leontine on the couch. She was more puzzled than alarmed. "What if it's a Domino's Pizza driver looking for directions?"

"Then I'll give him some. Meanwhile, I'll push the lock button behind me. Don't open the door for any reason unless you can see me through the window."

Insistent *rap-rap-rap* again.

"When I want back in, I'll knock twice quickly, then twice spaced a couple seconds apart. Don't even go to the window unless you hear that exact signal."

She sat up abruptly, jostling Jared, who didn't like it much but kept on sucking. "Who do you think it could be?"

"Could be Ed McMahon, but what immediately springs to mind is that, as a result of your interview last night, friend Gantt is making a move."

"What kind of move?" She was now seriously alarmed.

"An educational one."

"You're scaring the pee out of me. Why would you go outside if you think someone's waiting?"

"To do some schooling of my own."

Mo Zappatrane was, as Gantt had said, crazy. When still a high school sophomore, one Halloween he swallowed sixty-three goldfish. They didn't stay down, of course. Directly following the subsequent regurgitation, he'd rolled in the rancid puddle (much of which was still writhing, since he'd swallowed the fish whole), then went trick-or-treating for three hours without benefit of ablution. Or even a change of clothing. Claimed to be Vomit Monster. (His longtime acquaintances still blanch at the memory.)

And Mo's partner, Iggy Cremins, was indeed mean. Not long after his release from a fourth stint in prison—this one for grave robbing—Iggy had beaten his parole officer so badly with a lead kosh that the woman had never fully recovered. In fact, upon learning that she just *might* recover, he'd gone to her home and attacked her again, and for good measure placed her pet ferret in the microwave. (Three minutes on high.)

The pair thus made an imposing partnership, at least from the standpoint of mischief capability. Physically, they weren't quite so imposing. Iggy was six-four, on its own impressive enough, but he weighed only 161 pounds, which gave him shoulders like Howdy Doody. He still preferred a kosh, although now carried a leather one his mother had made for his thirtieth birthday, God rest her soul. It went almost thirty ounces, had a thong for his wrist, and the inscription *MOm* burned into one side with a wood-burning set. He also carried a SIG-Sauer .380 semi-automatic, but seldom used it since he loved the feel of bone crushing under his hand. A pistol at ten feet was too impersonal.

Mo, however, loved guns; he wore three all the time, except during his weekly shower. Then he just wore one. (Stainless steel, so it wouldn't rust.) Being all of five-feet-four when he stood straight (seldom), and matching Connor Gibbs almost pound for pound at 243, Mo wasn't exactly light on his feet. He thus moved only when he absolutely had to. During his halcyon puke-rolling years, he'd weighed a svelte 205. Sadly, those days were behind him, hence the three guns, which he used very well; any adversary caught in the open within fifty yards of Mo was in grave danger.

Right now, Mo had one of his guns in a clammy hand, and Iggy had his kosh, and Connor Gibbs was stepping through the trailer's front door and quietly closing it behind him.

• • •

When Connor descended from the mobile home, a pair of men stepped from the shadows to his left. One of them held something shiny black against his right leg; the other repeatedly slapped a poorly made kosh into a waiting palm. They stopped ten feet away, far too close for their own safety, though they didn't realize it since they were renowned more for mental aberration than mental acuity.

"Salvation Army?" Connor greeted.

Saurian brows beetled in confusion at the unexpected salutation, then, as the pair searched for a suitable rejoinder, Connor stepped forward and applied a fist to Mo's head—WHAP!—like that. The fist (slightly smaller than a bowling ball, but harder) impacted Mo's chunky chin, and out went the lights, though he did manage to hang onto his gun as his legs buckled and he sank to the ground. Iggy said "Hey!" and swung his kosh backhand, aiming for Connor's temple. Connor simply leaned back, let the blow pass, then swung his left arm up and over Iggy's right, continued the rolling counter-clockwise motion of his hand up under his opponent's armpit, then clamped his left elbow into his side, capturing Iggy's right arm and its now ineffectual kosh. Iggy, obviously figuring that when you've got a good line, you stick with it, said "Hey!" again and came up with his left, balling a fist. Too slow. Connor threw three lightning jabs—BAP!BAP!BAP!—while maintaining his hold on Iggy's arm. The pain to Iggy's elbow was excruciating, but not so much so that he didn't feel each wicked punch clear to his heels, his head snapping backward with each BAP! Nose bloodied, knees like Jell-O, Iggy tried desperately to fend off additional attention by waving his free hand in front of his face. Connor, using the captive arm as a lever and his own arm as the fulcrum, simply lifted Iggy high onto his toes, then directed the heel of his hand to the bridge of Iggy's battered nose.

And the fat lady sang.

•   •   •

Connor Gibbs collected four handguns, a homemade kosh with *MOm* on one side, a sap, two stilettos, and a can opener from the unconscious men at his feet, plus two wallets with no identification, an unopened pack of Luckies, and seventeen condoms. "Optimists," he said to himself, then knocked on the trailer door—twice fast, twice slow. The curtain moved; Leontine's chalky face appeared; her eyes widened; the door swung open.

"In ten minutes, call the cops," he said.

"Are you okay?" Still wide-eyed, but with the shotgun held purposefully in her small hands.

"Sure. Ten minutes, now. No sooner."

"Why so long?"

"I need to find out who sent these gentlemen."

"Think they'll tell you?"

Gibbs's grin was not unlike that of a great white shark upon spotting a seal in the water. "You bet," he said.

And they did. One of them, anyway. The other didn't regain consciousness for nearly half an hour.

Chapter 15

THE FIRST TWO CARS ON THE SCENE CARRIED uniforms and came careening down the crusty trailer park road as if en route to a Los Angeles bank heist. After screeching to a snow-spewing halt, from each car popped a cop, alert for overt moves or any semblance of same. At least their guns weren't drawn.

"Did you make the 911?" shouted the uniform nearest Connor Gibbs, who was now seated on the bottom step of Leontine's mobile home.

"Do I look like a Leontine Chevalier?" Connor returned.

"You needn't be flip, sir," said the second and farther uniform. "No one told us the caller's gender."

"I thought that was routine."

The second and farther cop, a tall red-haired drink of water, came over. "It usually is. This time they messed up. So who made the 911?"

Connor tossed a thumb over his shoulder. "She's in there."

The second and now closer cop glanced at the two blood-ied men sitting morosely off to one side, their backs against the trailer's foundation. "These the gents who occasioned the call?"

" 'Occasioned?' " said Connor.

"English minor," was the response, accompanied by a slow redheaded grin.

"Major in Mayhem?"

"Political Science. Plan to be governor. Soon."

"Those legs will get you plenty of votes."

The redhead, whose name tag read *Sherri Stonecipher,* said, "Can I count on it?" with a lazy long-legged look straight into Connor's eyes.

"As long as they mini-cam you full length."

"Hey!" Iggy interrupted the interchange. "I hate like hell to bother you, *Officer,* but that humongous sumbitch you're slapping gums with just gave me and my buddy a serious ass-whupping."

"Richly deserved, I suspect," said Sherri. She shrugged at Connor apologetically. "Duty calls."

"Some job," from Connor.

"Don't I know."

And then the plainclothes arrived.

"Estelle," said the short stocky detective, "you talk to the guy on the steps while I check out those goons Stonecipher has in tow."

"Sure," Estelle Lawson agreed, climbing out of the Chevy and walking over to Connor Gibbs, who did not get up. She stopped with her toes almost touching his. "You don't rise when a lady approaches, Mack?"

He looked up. "I'm tired. Those two slapped me around pretty good."

"I can tell. Move over," she ordered, and sat down beside him. Gibbs draped a heavy arm over her shoulders, kissed her cheek, and said, "How you been, Estelle?"

"Not so good. Larry left, you know."

"I heard. What, two months?"

"More like three, and unmarried life is rough. Singles bars, lovelorn ads in the paper, Sunday socials, unsafe sex."

Somebody wants to be with you.

Lucky # 2,9,22,23,24,44.

..is, famine, pestilence," he appended.

...ckled and squeezed his knee. "Ah, Connor. I've

...u. Heard from Cameron?"

...second lapse. She waited it out. Finally, he said,

...She makes it as hard for him as she can."

...should take him away."

...e's his mom, Estelle. He loves her. I wouldn't do that unless she were actually hurting him."

"Who knows what his being away from you is doing to him mentally."

Connor nodded. "I know. But he and I talk some. He's tough, and his heart's in the right place. Always has been. Cameron'll be okay." He was having difficulty speaking now.

"How about you? Will you be okay?"

"I don't matter."

"The hell you don't." Then they were quiet for a while, until she said, "So tell me about those creeps."

He did. All of it.

"You mean Helms was so offended by Ms. Chevalier's on-camera remark that he sent Mutt and Jeff over with a lesson in manners." She shook her head. "Male ego."

"Watch out."

"Not you, hon, not you. Autonomy isn't ego." She stood up. "Call me?"

"For some unsafe sex?"

"Any kind you want."

He grinned up at her.

"No joke, Connor, call sometime. Mustn't forget your friends."

He took her hand and rubbed it with his cheek. Estelle looked at the mobile home. "That woman sure has had her share of troubles. First the husband, then her son . . ." She looked back at Connor. "Now this. You bust those guys up proper?"

He shook his head. "Not bad. I did have to massage the

scrawny one some to squeeze out a little information, but it won't show."

She patted his arm. "Same old Connor. You take care," she said, and went to meet Leontine.

"So the two of you were just sitting here talking when a rap came at the door, like something out of Poe," said the short stocky detective, his Bic poised above a ratty notebook.

"And feeding the baby," corrected Leontine over the rim of her coffee cup, steam veiling her dark eyes.

The detective arched his brows suggestively. "Breast-feeding, with this lug in the room?"

"I never said—" Leontine began, but Connor interrupted.

"You covered this, Detective, and you took notes. Refer to them."

Short-and-stocky tossed Gibbs a look. "How about you let me do my job in my own way?"

"Then drop the innuendos."

Estelle jumped in, asking Connor, "Why did you go to the door instead of her?"

"Because of the TV interview yesterday, and the fact that she wasn't expecting visitors."

"And you didn't see anyone outside," from the dumpy detective.

"Right."

"But you went out anyway."

"Right."

"Looking for trouble?"

"Santa Claus," Connor said.

"So these two guys come around the corner . . . from which way did you say?"

"My left."

"Oh, yeah. Got it right here." The plump detective pointed to his notes, then glanced back up, smirking. "And then they attacked you."

"The tall one took a swing."

"With what?"

"A leather kosh, like I told you. Check your notes again."

"Oh, yeah, here it is." He smiled at Gibbs, relishing the role of irritating interrogator. Connor looked at Estelle, whose body language said, *Sorry, but he's in charge.* The pudgy cop caught the brief visual exchange, interpreted it, and scowled. "Got a problem, Estelle?"

"Nope."

"I do," said Connor, standing. "You've overstayed your welcome."

The stocky dick also climbed to his feet, all five-feet-eight of him. "What, you gonna grab me by the scruff of my neck and toss me out?"

"No, but I might call your captain, downtown. Get you out of my hair."

"I could arrest you, then you can talk to him face to face."

"And the charge?"

"How about felonious assault?"

Gibbs laughed out loud.

Face dangerously red—from the combined effects of alcohol abuse and unmedicated high blood pressure—the detective said, "Those guys claim they were lost, just stopped to use the phone. Claim you popped them in the chops with no warning."

Leontine erupted. "That's ridiculous!"

"He knows that," said Connor. "So arrest me, Detective. Or get the hell out."

The short stocky cop stood there, angry but not uncertain; he was bluffing and he knew Connor knew it.

"Right now," Gibbs said, the timbre of his voice changing.

Estelle noticed and, knowing Connor as she did, recognized the threat and climbed to her feet. "We have all we need, and we've bothered these people enough. Let's go."

The chunky policeman, reluctant to give ground, did so with a parting shot. "Maybe we'll meet again."

"I'll look forward to it," said Connor Gibbs.

"Don't ever do that," said the male detective en route to their squad car.

"Do what?" asked Estelle.

"Undermine my authority in front of a perp."

She snorted. "Connor's no perp."

The short stocky cop stopped in his tracks and took Estelle's arm roughly. "Did you hear what I said?"

"Let go the arm," she warned.

He squeezed tighter.

"I won't tell you again, I'll just knee your balls up around your tonsils."

He gave her a lupine grin and squeezed even tighter. "Yeah?"

She kneed his crotch, very hard and very fast, the point of her patella taking him precisely on the scrotum. Releasing her arm, he sagged to the ground and swayed there on all fours, like a sick elephant, head hanging, the waves of pain and nausea overwhelming.

Estelle knelt beside him with one hand on his back, patting gently. "Breathe easy, it'll pass." She remained beside him, soothing. When the worst was over and he was ready to stand, she held him in place with the soothing hand. "Oh, two things, partner. One, never take your frustrations out on me. Two, don't ever touch me again, even if I need CPR. Got it?"

He nodded, so she helped him up.

While the short stocky detective was outside getting his balls shoved up around his tonsils, Connor Gibbs was inside phoning Richard Abernathy, a local fence.

"Yo!" said Abernathy.

"This is Connor Gibbs."

"Yo."

"We need to do some business. Tonight."

"Yo?"

"You know the trailer park on Highway 64, just south of Wendover?"

"Yo."

"Seventh trailer on the left. Out front is a blue Pacer."

"I'm buying a car?"

"No, small stuff. Bring cash."

"Yo."

"Eleven-thirty. We're getting ready to watch *Miracle on 34th Street*."

"Maureen O'Hara?"

"The new one."

"Ain't as good."

"I know, I've seen it. She hasn't."

"My kids think the new one's better, but what do they know? You said she?"

"She."

"Yours?"

"I work for her."

"She a looker?"

"Not your type."

"Ain't got no pussy, huh," Abernathy said, and hung up.

"Was that a friend of yours?" Leontine asked as Connor hung up the phone and walked over to the VCR.

"A business acquaintance. He has a nude carwash, a gentleman's club, an adult book store, a wife, five kids, and a half-dozen mistresses that I know of."

"Isn't he a prince!"

Gibbs shrugged. "He's reliable, and he loves three things." He poked the movie into the VCR.

"And they are?"

"Money and his family."

"That's two things."

He looked at her.

"Oh. Will I have to disinfect the place after he's gone?"

"He's clean enough, externally."

"Why invite him over here?"

"Business."

"Couldn't you go to his place?"

He sat on the couch, put his feet up. "He doesn't have a place, not in the sense you mean."

"So he's coming here. To my home. With my child sleeping right down the hall."

Connor nodded just as the preview for *Dunston Checks In* appeared on the screen. The irrepressible chimp, dressed like Santa, was hanging upside down from a chimney.

Leontine pointed at the TV and said, "Is that Abernathy?"

"Too cute, but about the right size," Connor replied.

Then they watched the movie.

Abernathy wore faded jeans with holes at the knees and a Stones sweatshirt with mustard stains on the left sleeve not far from a Rolex President. A navy Greek fisherman's cap topped an unruly thatch of flaxen hair; his leather brogans had last seen polish just before Reagan's reelection. At five-feet-seven and 145 pounds, he was not physically imposing, but some claimed he had more money than Steve Forbes. Leontine sat in the rocker with a copy of *Handling Sin* in her lap, a forefinger marking her place. Abernathy stood by the door, appraising her as if she were a commodity.

"Ms. Chevalier, Mr. Abernathy," introduced Connor from the entrance to the hall.

"Pleased to meet you, Mr. Abernathy," said Leontine.

"I'm Rich."

"Never tell it by the way you dress."

He laughed at that. "You always so rude?"

Leontine stood with her book. "Only to men."

"He's a man." Abernathy indicated Connor.

"Only on the outside," she quipped, and left them alone.

Watching her sway down the hall, carnality oozing from his every pore, Abernathy said, "There goes a fox."

"Let's get to it."

"What you got?"

Connor pointed to the kitchen table, whereon lay Iggy's SIG .380 and Mo's Beretta Tomcat, Smith & Wesson stainless .357 snub, and a Coonan in the same chambering, plus two Italian stilettos and a can opener. Abernathy gave them a quick once-over and announced, "Thirty-five cents for the church key. Everything else is junk."

"Take notes," Connor began. "I want a new or like-new VCR, 4-head, stereo, with remote. Christmas tree, Fraser fir, no less than seven feet. Assorted ornaments, nothing chintzy, and tinsel. Star or angel for the crest. New clothes and toys for a six-month-old boy, separate boxes, all wrapped. Nice, no paper you can see through. And a grand. Cash. Now."

"Connor, Connor, Connor," Rich whined. "There's not a chance in the world them four pieces ain't hot, which means they'd best leave the state, or go to some part of town money don't grow on trees. The SIG'll fetch three, maybe four, but nobody wants revolvers anymore, so the Smith is a bust. And—"

"Rich?" Gibbs interrupted. "The Sig will bring five since it's stainless, and you know it. And the Smith two or better, revolver or not. The Tomcat's hot right now, since it's new on the market. Try to find one in a gunshop."

"Nobody but winos want a .32, man. It's a pipsqueak."

"Maybe, but it'll fit into a jock and hits harder than a .25. The cops are keen on it right now for a back-up piece. It'll bring two, two-and-a-half."

"I don't sell to cops, and most of my regular clients wear clothes you could conceal a SAM under. Nobody wants a .32. The Coonan's got a reputation for jamming with hollow-point ammunition, and—"

"Richard?"

"Yo?"

"Quit sparring. Either you cough up what I said or I'll call Fob Blackwood."

"Fob won't give you jack shit for this batch! Besides, when did he ever—"

"It's late."

Abernathy sighed, the weight of the world obviously on his former welterweight shoulders. Right. The truth was he'd reap twice his cash outlay before the night was over, and they both knew it. From a pants pocket he pulled a roll of bills. A thick roll. All hundreds. Peeling off eight, he offered them to Connor, who shook his head. Another Abernathy sigh, then two more bills left the roll. Connor accepted those, along with the first eight. "Get a woman to choose the ornaments," he instructed. "Your wife, if she's still speaking to you."

"Gladys? She loves me, man. When you need the stuff?"

"As soon as. Don't bring me a 2-head, or one with no remote. And remember, new or like-new."

"I don't renege on deals," Abernathy responded, scooping up the armament. "We done?"

"A pleasure," Connor said, holding out a hand.

"As always." They shook, Abernathy left, and Connor went to make tea.

Leontine lay in bed, wide awake, pondering. Was tonight a good time to make her move? Had she known Connor long enough? Would this scare him off? No way; she'd never heard of a man who would turn down no-strings sex, except maybe Jerry Falwell, and she wasn't sure about him.

What did she have to lose?

Connor's help.

Shit. She hated making critical decisions.

• • •

Gibbs felt the cot move and a naked body mold itself to his. He rolled onto his back, the cot barely holding the two of them. Leontine ran slender fingers through his chest hair, trailed a provocative nail down his belly, traced a figure eight around his navel. Instant turgidity, despite himself.

"Hi," she breathed into an ear, increasing the blood flow to a specific organ.

"What are you doing, Leontine?"

"Inviting you to my bed."

"Well, this one sure isn't big enough for both of us."

Throaty laugh, same ear. Priapus, dear Priapus. The arousing finger headed south.

"Whoa," he said, voice cracking.

"Your body isn't saying whoa," she argued, reaching between his legs and filling her hand. To overflowing. Her breath caught on its way from lungs to lips. He didn't stir. Well, most of him didn't, anyway.

"Wow," she whispered, stroking, squeezing.

"Thanks, but I'll pass."

The words jarred her. "What the hell does that mean?"

"That I won't allow this to continue."

She smiled up at him. "You sure you can stop?"

"I'm sure."

Sitting up abruptly, her small breasts absorbing the soft light from the window, she said angrily, "How can you be so sure? It's obvious I turn you on."

He lifted his head to look at himself swaying in the moonlight. "Obvious is right. Can excessive tumescence be terminal?"

She couldn't help but giggle. "How do you know when it's excessive?"

"Did you see *Cocoon*?"

"Yeah, why?"

"Remember the love scene in the pool?"

Brow knit from concentration, she said, "Not clearly."

"As I recall, Guttenberg's line was 'If this is foreplay, I'm a dead man.'"

She grinned. "Sounds right."

"Pinch me, see if I'm still alive."

She did, causing him to jump.

"I didn't mean *there!*" he protested.

"It was all I could reach." Abruptly serious, she sat up and pulled the blanket around herself. "Would you mind explaining?"

"I never have sex with someone I'm working with."

"Why?"

"It doesn't work."

She absorbed that, and his dour demeanor. "Bitter experience talking?"

He nodded. "Very bitter."

"What happened to her?"

"She died."

The impact of that silenced Leontine for a moment. Presently she asked, "Will you tell me?"

"On a job, years ago, for the government—never mind the specifics—I fell for one of the other . . . one of my partners. Bad case of head-over-heels. It affected my judgment. Turned out she was a double.

"We had just finished . . . you know . . . and I'd fallen asleep beside her. She had bladder problems, so frequently got up to use the bathroom during the night. I'd grown used to it and didn't normally wake up. On this particular night, she went to the toilet as usual, but to get a knife she'd taped to the bottom of the tank. She was about to slit my throat with it when a member of my team intervened. He had been suspicious of her from the start."

"Intervened?"

"He shot her."

"I'm sorry." Leontine stood by the cot. "I apologize for bringing back a painful memory."

"You didn't know."

Trying to make light of an awkward moment, she pointed to his lower appendage, now retired. "At least that problem seems to be resolved."

He looked down, then back up at her, mild regret lurking in his eyes. "Then get out of here before it reasserts itself."

"*Reasserts itself.* I like that," she said, simpering. "I really do affect you, don't I?"

He stood, took her by the shoulders, and kissed her forehead. "You're as sexy as hell, and I like you. Of course you affect me. If you weren't employing me . . ."

"Maybe when it's over?"

"Who knows. You may not want to then."

"I will," she promised blithely, but internally she was seething.

Her plan had failed.

Connor lay on his cot, wide awake. The old wound, which he had thought long healed, was reopened . . .

In his mind's eye lay Tabitha, on the floor with a hole in her forehead and a knife in her hand and a wide-eyed look of surprise on her lovely face . . .

. . . that beautiful, stone-dead face . . .

Connor had been so enraged it took four very tough men to subdue him, and he'd broken the jaw of one of them . . .

A man whose life Connor had saved on more than one occasion . . .

A man who, upon killing Tabitha, the double agent, had unquestionably saved Connor's life . . .

A man who, years later, Connor asked to be godfather to his own son, Cameron . . .

The man was Holmes Crenshaw, attorney at law.

Chapter 16

"THEY HERE?" HE ASKED, DIPPING HIS BRUSH into the pigment.

"Yes, sir. They are out by the pool."

"Plenty of suds?"

"Certainly, sir."

"Send Marvin for the Jewel," said Gantt Helms.

"Right away, sir," from the butler, who looked like Odd Job without the derby.

Helms continued to paint until it was *juuuust* right. "There!" he exclaimed, satisfied. Before him on the canvas was Tinkerbell, doing the macarena. It was very lifelike, because he was very good. When Marvin came in with the Jewel, Gantt tossed his brush toward the bench; it caromed off, landed on the carpet, and deposited a green smear. Helms couldn't have cared less; countless stains sullied the area already. "Have Choi clean up this fucking mess," he ordered.

"Sir!" answered Marvin, a former marine dog handler, as they headed for the large heated indoor pool.

Iggy and Mo were there, seated in deck chairs, with concerned looks on their faces and Coors in their fists. Manning and Sherman sat well away from the duo, distancing themselves from the storm. Beside Sherman, on the tiled floor, fully, absolutely, perilously alert, sat Bingo, an Alsatian the size of a Shetland pony. Iggy and Mo, having for fifteen minutes been subjected to Bingo's immutable stare as they sucked down brew after brew, now nervously noted an infinitely more ominous presence.

Shit! they thought simultaneously.

"Hi, fellas," greeted their employer, padding over to his own king-sized chair. "How's it hanging?"

"Fine, Boss," from Mo, foam on his lips; he'd just opened a fresh can, but most of it was now on his shoe.

"Yeah, just fine," agreed Iggy, a bit falsetto.

"Doing okay, then?" said Gantt, the picture of amiability, with the Jewel lying beside him on a purple velvet pillow.

"Yeah, fine," assured the pair.

His face a model of concern, Helms asked, "Then that jazzbo at the trailer park didn't rough you up too bad?"

"Naw," said Mo. "Didn't even hit me but once."

Iggy, crazy but not dumb, said nothing.

Brows arched incredulously, Gantt said, "Just once? How come Iggy's face looks like he head-butted a train? Bet he got hit more than once."

"I got knocked out right away," Mo explained. "Don't remember nothing else."

"I heard that. I also heard that when you come to, this Gibbs guy asked you a few questions."

"Yeah," Mo reported. "But I didn't tell him nuthin'!"

"So I got nothing to worry about, right?"

Manning shifted uneasily. Sherman simply waited. Bingo watched Mo and Iggy.

"Right," agreed Mo, seeing light at the end of the tunnel.

"Wrong! JEWEL!" The flabby arm came up, middle finger extended. Toward Mo.

Like a leopard, Jewel sprang, canines bared, taking Mo not only unexpectedly, but by the front of the neck, powerful jaws closing, ripping, twisting from side to side. The deck chair went over backward, combatants along with it, blood spewing. Mo, heels drumming the tiles in panic, tried to scream.

He couldn't.

His voice box had disappeared down Jewel's throat.

Bingo hadn't moved a muscle.

Iggy neither.

Task completed, Jewel recrossed the room to resume her place beside Master.

Manning gulped a major dose of Bacardi.

Marvin scratched his nose and yawned.

Sherman went over to prod Mo's still-twitching remains with a toe. "Jeepers, little brother. Shoulda put down a drop cloth."

Using a damp towel, Gantt Helms wiped the Jewel's muzzle free of arterial scarlet. The Tosa-Fila sat placidly.

Bingo still hadn't moved a muscle.

Iggy neither.

Gantt said, "We on the same page here, Iggy."

Iggy, completely immobile, except for his lips, replied, "You bet."

"Any comments about your pal Mo?"

"Never did like him."

Gantt nodded. "Okay. Now, listen up. You get sent out on a job again, don't fuck it up."

"Right," agreed Iggy, still as a wart.

"Now get the hell out. Marvin, put the Jewel back. Give her a couple extra T-bones. After she eats, check if her teeth need cleaning."

"Sir, yes, sir!" Marvin acknowledged.

"JEWEL!" barked Helms, pointing to the door. Jewel preceded Marvin to her heated and very large cage.

"You still here?" Gantt Helms asked of Iggy Cremins.

"That dog ain't took its eyes off me," he explained, tilting his chin toward the Alsatian. "I'm scared to move."

Gantt climbed to his fat flat feet. "Shiiiuut, Old Bingo wouldn't hurt a gerbil. Unless I told him to. Sherm, have Choi clean up this fucking mess. BINGO! HEEL!"

Bingo heeled. As they left poolside, Gantt was singing:

"Bee—eye—in—gee—oh!

"Bee—eye—in—gee—oh!

"Bee—eye—in—gee—oh!

"And Bingo was his name-oh!"

Chapter 17

"I REALLY APPRECIATE THE MONEY," LEONTINE said. "You have no idea how bad I needed it, and what I can do with it. A thousand dollars. I can have the car fixed."

"You're welcome," from Connor Gibbs, halting for a closer look. Leontine, holding Jared, stopped beside him.

"Why are you examining those potatoes so closely?"

"Looking for cuts and bruises. Checking the tint."

"Tint as in color?"

"As in."

Leontine shifted Jared to her other slender hip. "Aren't potatoes just brown?"

"Russet potatoes sometimes show a greenish tinge, from alkaloid buildup. Makes them bitter," said Connor, placing a half dozen ungreen potatoes into a clear plastic bag, spinning it, securing with a twist tie. "These will do nicely."

"How do they get what-you-said buildup?"

"Exposure to light."

"You planning to bake those?"

"Mash them."

"What if I don't want mashed potatoes?"

"Pass them up." He moved on down the aisle.

"Why do you get to cook for Mr. Crenshaw. What if I wanted to?"

Pausing, Connor said, "Do you want to?"

"I said what if."

"If you decide to, holler. I'll let you choose the victuals."

Jared began to fret. Damp diaper. Gibbs said, "You want me to change him?"

"I can do it, Connor. I read how in a book."

"Just offering."

"I can take care of him too, you know. He *is* my son, even if you do spend more time with him than I do."

Connor was taken aback. "My, aren't we testy."

In lieu of response, she whirled and stalked off to the restroom. Connor resumed foraging. Leeks, carrots, celery, two medium-sized zucchini, one large onion, tomatoes. Garlic, thyme leaves, basil leaves, pepper for grinding, parsley. Pearl barley, lentils, Famous Amos oatmeal raisin cookies, on sale. Leontine rejoined him as he nabbed Amos. "Get me some chocolate-chip-pecan, will you? I'll pay for them."

He grabbed a box, saying, "Any olive oil at your place?"

"Only on TV."

"Beg your pardon?"

"Popeye."

He laughed, aware that she was trying to regain her footing and wanting to make it easy for her.

"I'm sorry," she tendered.

"As Holmie would say, no prob."

"I was being a bitch."

"I said no problem."

"Let me finish."

"Just forget the whole thing, not that there's really anything to forget. I suppose I do monopolize Jared, so I should be the one apologizing.

"Oh, sure. You should apologize for all the cooking and cleaning and diaper changing and feeding and burping, not to mention beating the shit out of two men who came to beat the shit out of me. Yeah, Connor, you have a lot to apologize for."

"But I enjoy cooking and feeding and burping, and can endure cleaning and soiled diapers without permanent trauma."

She glanced sideways at him as he pushed the cart. "What about the fighting?"

"I don't enjoy that."

"Well, you're sure good at it."

He shrugged.

"Come clean, here. You don't get a kick out of smashing your fist into some crud's nose?" Jared pulled her hair, so she shifted him to where his little hands wouldn't reach.

"How did I know they were cruds?"

"They came over to—"

"We don't know for certain why they came. Maybe they'd been told to scare you."

"But you told me—"

"I know what I told you. And they most likely did intend to do more than frighten. My point is, how could I know that? The reason I took them on was that they had weapons out and obviously intended to use them." He fell silent momentarily, then went on.

"I was kicked off my high school football team in my senior year, because I wasn't aggressive enough for the coach. 'Maim the quarterback!' he'd say. '*Hurt* him!' All I'd do was tackle. I led the state in sacks, but the coach said I was a wuss, that I didn't have that 'killer instinct.' He was right, at least . . ."

She waited, but he was not forthcoming. "At least what?"

"At least when it came to sports," he said, and turned a corner.

"What are we having, *Sufi*?" asked Holmes Crenshaw, attorney at law, sniffing the air.

"Sauteed squid, rutabaga casserole, steamed artichokes, french fries," Connor replied from the kitchen, where he was creating a myriad of delightful aromas.

"He's lying," Leontine said.

"You bet," agreed the solicitor. "He knows I hate french fries."

"You don't like french fries?" from Leontine. "I don't believe I've ever met anyone who didn't like fries."

"When we were kids," Connor dissented, "Holmes worked at McDonald's. He *lived* on fries. Then one night, after a particularly wild party—during which he drank more than his share—we stopped at Mickey Dee's on the way home. He stuffed his gullet with three large orders of greasy—"

"Please, not right before we eat," Holmes pleaded.

". . . fries, then staggered back out to his 396 Chevelle and we headed home. Although not exactly sober, I was nowhere near as drunk as Holmes. Nonetheless, I ran a stop sign and drew a statey. He put me through a sobriety test while our future barrister here groaned loudly in the back seat. Eventually, Smokey stuck his head inside the car to see what all the noise was about. Holmes's response was a bout of projectile vomiting, with the officer on the receiving end."

Enjoying this, Leontine said, "Well? What happened?"

"I spent a miserable night in jail with *Sufi* here and forswore french fries forever," finished Crenshaw.

"And so far as I know, he's never eaten one since."

"What's *Sufi*?" Leontine asked Holmes Crenshaw.

"An Arab friend of Connor's used to call him that. He alleged it meant 'wise one.' "

Leontine nodded and chewed. "This is delicious."

"Thanks," Connor acknowledged.

"It's one of his specialties, and one of my favorites,"

Holmes elaborated. "Stewed lentils, barley, and vegetables. Got the recipe from an old guy in Budapest, one of our top operatives. I remember one time when he—"

"More tea?" Connor said pointedly.

"No thanks, still have plenty. Once he—"

"Bread?" Connor insisted.

Holmes pointed with his knife. "Got bread. There was this time—"

"Mr. Crenshaw, I don't think Connor wants to talk about this," observed Leontine.

Holmes looked at his friend. "No?"

"No."

Holmes put a chunk of potato in his mouth. "Whyever not?" Then, responding to the look on Connor's face, he countered with, "Never mind. What shall we discuss?"

Dipping a spoon into his pudding, Gibbs said, "Since the charges against Leontine were dropped, can you get her gun back?"

"I suppose so, if I pursue it. But you know how things tend to get lost in the evidence room. Especially guns and dope."

"Not money?" from Leontine.

"Oddly, no," said Holmes, sipping tea. "They keep records on that. What kind of gun?"

"Won't it be tagged with her name?"

Crenshaw looked at Connor pityingly. "Who at the station can write?"

"It's a .38 Special," Leontine offered helpfully. "I know because I had to buy bullets for it once."

"There are lots of .38 Specials," said the lawyer. "Do you know the brand?"

Characteristically, Leontine's brow knit as she concentrated. "It's like the hospital."

"What hospital?" from Holmes.

Connor said, "Charter?"

"That's it!" agreed Leontine excitedly.

Crenshaw said, "Charter Arms. How big is it?"

She held her hands a few inches apart. "Like so."

"Is the barrel short?"

"About the same as the rest of the gun."

"How many rounds does it hold?" Connor asked.

"Rounds? Oh, bullets. Six."

To himself, Connor said, "Not the Undercover." Then to Holmes: "That enough for you to go on?"

"Six-shot Charter Arms with a four-inch barrel. Piece of cake, assuming it hasn't grown legs."

Short pause while everyone continued eating, then Crenshaw asked, "You think she might need it?"

"Probably not," was Connor's answer. But he didn't look convinced.

Holmes Crenshaw had gone home, Jared was down, and the shower was on. Leontine stood in the hallway. *Should I be subtle?* she pondered. *Candlelight, wine, dim lights, Johnny Mathis, negligee? Sure, that ought to work,* she smiled self-effacingly. *After all, he only lives in a three-hundred-thousand-dollar house—beside a freaking golf course, no less—while I have this terrific trailer.* She almost laughed out loud. *I can't afford wine, for Pete's sake, and my stereo's busted, so I guess Johnny is out. I've never owned a negligee because Big Sam didn't seem to need one.* She paused, remembering what had always turned Sam on, like flipping a switch.

The shower still ran. *Why not give it one more shot?* she decided.

Removing her clothes, she eased open the bathroom door. Swirling steam enveloped her as she pushed back the curtain to climb in with Connor Gibbs.

"Here, let me wash your back," she said, taking the Dial from his hand.

He jumped. "That's not my back."

"By golly, you're right. I'll wash it anyway."

"Leontine?"

"Hmmm?"

"This can't continue. I'll blow a gasket."

"Or something."

He turned to her. She continued to scrub.

"Leontine. This can *not* continue."

She smiled and washed faster, there now being more area to cover.

He removed her hands, rinsed free of soap, climbed out of the tub. Leontine finished bathing alone. When she stepped onto the floor five minutes later, Connor came into the bathroom fully dressed, his hair still damp. "I loaded the shotgun and put it beside your bed," he said. "I'll see you in a few hours. Don't open the door for anyone. Not even Marlene."

"Where are you going?" she said crossly, irritated at this second rebuff.

"Out."

"Out where?"

"See you in a few hours," he repeated, and left.

"Bennie here," she said into the phone.

"You free?" he said from his end.

"I'm cheap, but I'm not free."

"I need to see you."

"I'm tired, sugar pie. Had three one-hour classes tonight. I was fixing to bathe and turn in."

"I *really* need to see you," Connor pleaded.

Huge sigh from her end. "A woman's work is never done. Do I have time to shower?"

"I'm on cellular. Be there in five minutes if I hit the lights right."

"Then I'll just turn down the bed and drape my naked

body across it seductively. Or perhaps slip into that tiny black thing you bought me last—"

"Bennie, I'm ready to howl at the moon as it is."

"Poor baby. Maybe I'll shave, too, here and there," she whispered.

He shut off the phone and drove faster.

Chapter 18

BENELLA MAE SWEET HAD LIVED A TOUGH LIFE. Reared primarily in an orphanage until she was ten, she had moved in with a maternal aunt and step-uncle. She blossomed early, and it nearly ruined her life; her step-uncle viewed the blossoming as if it were just for him. When she was eleven, he and a cousin tied Benella to her bed and took their pleasure, repeatedly, for twelve hours, damaging her so badly that it would prevent her from ever bearing children. She ran away to Memphis, where she was taken in off the streets by a kindly old lady—who promptly turned her over to a New Orleans pimp for five thousand dollars. Benella was forced to turn tricks for nearly six months, by which time she was so strung out on illegal substances that she was rendered unsuitable as an object of fornication for pay. Ever resourceful, the pimp stuck her in a French Quarter peep show house to perform blowjobs through a hole cut in the wall, at five bucks a pop. She stayed there three months. Then one sunflower afternoon she used her overseer's serrated-blade pocket knife to cut the femoral arteries in both his legs as he lay in a drunken stupor, gelding him for good measure. He bled to death with satisfactory alacrity, screaming and writhing all the while. Benella then hitch-hiked back to Memphis, looked up the little old lady who had sold her into bondage. They talked things over. For six hours. In the old lady's basement. Where the neighbors wouldn't hear. It turned out that the old biddy had peddled more than three hundred girls over a twenty-year period. Well. She'd never sell another. The body wasn't discovered for seven weeks, since the little old lady had no friends.

To support her drug habit, Benella gained weight, bought some clothes with money appropriated from her former pimp, and put herself back on the street, as sole proprietress. Having no pimp to protect her, she was often beaten by her customers, once so severely she nearly lost the vision in her left eye. One night, while looking to score some smack out of a bar in a particularly unsavory neighborhood, a former client—the one who had damaged her eye—spotted her and decided to renew their relationship. She spurned his offer, not being desirous of his abusive company again at any price, but he repugned her right of refusal. An argument ensued, and the jerk began to pummel her savagely, to the entertainment of a throng of onlookers.

Benella fought valiantly, but was no match for her antagonist, who knocked her down twice, picked up a bottle, broke it on the edge of the bar, and announced his intention to cut off one of her ears. She braced herself, but the carving never took place. Suddenly, the bottle-wielder was grabbed from behind by a very large man who had just entered the bar in search of an FBI informant named Manteo Murf. Upon seeing the hapless girl cowering on the floor—and her tormentor brandishing a bottle, obviously preparing to operate—the huge fellow had gone berserk. When the melee was over, the bottle man had four broken bones, five fewer teeth, and lacerations requiring sixty-seven stitches to close.

Connor Gibbs, Benella's savior, arranged for medical treatment and subsequent rehab, and a stay in a battered women's shelter. Over the next six years, he provided her with funds, food, shelter, clothing, schooling, and 46 rock CDs. She wrote him a thank you note for each CD. Her aversion to males was so understandably strong that she took only one lover during all those years, an older woman, one of her high school English teachers, safely married, thus lessening any chance of acquiring HIV. The teacher, not yet out of the closet, desired children and fully intended to stay married. Neither the teacher nor Benella was promiscuous, so the two had a fine relationship.

In appreciation for all Gibbs had done, when Benella graduated from college she set out to repay her benefactor in the time-honored way. Connor was reluctant at first, but she was persistent—and incredibly attractive. Having matured to six-feet-one and 173 pounds, with hair the color of wheat straw and the physical presence of a tigress, Benella was indeed hard to resist. Eventually, Connor ceased trying. They became intimate. The fact that Benella was involved with a woman had no effect on either of them, nor on the woman in question.

Benella's BA in business gelled nicely with her longtime interest in fitness. Connor fronted her the money to open a gym, which was an immediate success. Now, ten years later, it continued to be. Once she was financially secure, Benella repaid every penny of Connor's original investment. She still taught aerobics classes, enabling her to maintain impressive size while keeping a body fat level below fourteen percent. Busty, tawny-skinned, with legs clear up to her chin and a face that halted men in their tracks, Benella Mae Sweet was smart, well-educated, witty, good-humored, politically active. And Connor Gibbs's best friend.

At the moment, she reached across his groin with a long, slender, cleanly muscled limb to snag the top sheet with prehensile toes and pull it across their entwined nakedness. "Whew! You weren't kidding, were you?" she proclaimed.

Connor moaned in response.

"Like it when I shave, don't you, cuddly?" she teased.

He moaned again.

"I never shave for anyone but you, you know that?" she whispered.

He pivoted his head from side to side where it lay between her breasts.

"Not even JoAnn," she assured.

He nodded in appreciation.

"I'm eight to your two. Want to go for the gold?" she challenged.

"I thought you were tired," he mumbled.

"I'm never *that* tired," she insisted, letting her fingers do the walking.

When he staggered from her door at dawn, the score was fifteen to three.

Her favor.

Chapter 19

Leontine Chevalier was in her bedroom asleep, and Connor was at her kitchen table munching a handful of mazzards, when a knock came at the door. Richard Abernathy, bearing gifts: an eight-foot Fraser fir, full and symmetrical; half a dozen boxes of assorted ornaments, expensive; six strings of multicolored lights, new and unwrapped; tinsel and strings of popcorn; both a star *and* an angel, in original containers; eighteen gaily wrapped packages, various sizes and shapes; twenty one-hundred dollar bills, in an envelope—unlicked, so Connor could count it. Abernathy wore faded camos with holes at both knees, a Stones T-shirt with ketchup stains on its right sleeve, a Patek Phillippe on his left wrist, and a Chicago Bulls cap on his only head. "You done good, Richard," said Connor. "But what's the extra money for?"

Abernathy waxed sheepish. "Told the wife about the situation. She insisted."

Connor grinned. "God bless her."

"Hey, don't let this give you notions. It's a one-shot deal. Besides," he grinned back, "it's Christmas. And she's got the kid, you know?"

Gibbs nodded. "You're okay in my book, no matter what everyone says."

"Yeah, well just don't let it get around," Abernathy said and left. The phone rang as he was tooling off in his big Dodge van with the sky darkening overhead.

Connor said, "Hello."

"Don Quixote, please."

"Hiya, Pop."

"Haven't seen you in two weeks."

"I know, and I apologize."

"You still tall?"

"Not compared to Kareem Abdul Jabbar."

"Still ugly?"

"I look like you."

"The mailman. Your mother tells me you're living in sin with some woman named Maurice Chevalier."

"If so, it doesn't live up to its billing."

"No frenzied bouts of copulation?"

"No, but we took a shower together once. Kind of."

"Cleanliness is good."

"I hate to be rude, Dad, but ah, did you want something?"

"Since when do you mind being rude? Blister's been trying to reach you."

"I'll give him a call."

"Ever hear of answering machines?"

"Now that you mention it."

"So why don't you get one?"

"Then people would leave me messages. Maybe Ed McMahon, telling me I didn't win. Again."

"Like you need the money. You're in the sixty percent tax bracket now."

"There is no sixty percent bracket. Yet. And look who's talking."

"So I'm well heeled. I'm not ashamed of it."

"Or anything else. Can I call Blister now?"

"Be kind to your old man. Someday, I'll be incontinent and senile."

"Someday?"

"Bye, ape."

"Love you, Pop."

"And watch those showers . . ." Then he hung up.

Cody Wainwright McGraw, more commonly known as Blister, lived with his Aunt Vera—who had adopted him at age three—and a Boykin spaniel named Zepper, a gift from Gibbs. It being Saturday, Blister was home when Connor phoned. "Hiya, Spud," greeted Gibbs.

"Connor! I tried your office, then your house, three times apiece, and you weren't anywhere. So I called Mr. Walter. Hope he didn't mind."

"He didn't."

"Did you ever think about getting an answering machine?"

"Someone else asked me that recently."

"Well? Did you?"

"I thought about it once."

"And?"

"Decided against it."

"Why?"

"I knew you'd fill up the tape."

"Aw, Connor . . ."

"What can I do for you, buddy?"

"Aunt Vera rented *The Relic*. Have you seen it?"

"In the theater, some years ago."

"You take Bennie?"

"She took me."

"Wanna watch it tonight?"

"You clear it with Vera?"

"She won't mind. She's got a date, anyway."

"If she okays it, I'll pick you up around six, and we'll snag a pizza and scope the flick."

"Do what?"

"Know you not street vernacular, boy?"

"Street what?"

"Argot."

"Connor, if I live to be a hundred—"

"You'll understand me only half the time, right?"

"No. I'll be a *very old man.*" The boy was still laughing when Connor rang off.

Leontine Chevalier was awed by the array of Christmas goodies, but still grumpy about her unsuccessful shower seduction. "You might have checked with me first," she groused.

"About the Christmas stuff?"

"No, about Blister coming over to watch a movie."

"I suppose I should have at that, but it never occurred to me that you'd mind. Well, we can all go over to my house, and you can watch whatever you want in the upstairs bedroom."

"Why can't I watch a movie downstairs, and you *boys* take the bedroom?"

"Because the downstairs TV has surround. *The Relic* relies heavily on sound, plus some fair special effects, since the script isn't much."

"What if I don't want to go to your house?"

"Promise me you won't run out and kill Gantt Helms tonight, and I'll leave you here alone."

"Helms sent his goons after *me,* remember?"

"Yes. But you hired me to keep you from acing him, not the other way around."

"Does it make a difference?"

"You bet. If my job were to protect you from Helms, I'd go about it differently."

"How?"

"I'd take the game to him."

She thought about that, the implications. Maybe she could find a use for Gibbs yet, in a way similar to what she'd originally envisioned. Time to be nice: "Okay. We can stay here. I'll even watch your dumb old movie if you'll let me put Jared down first. Did you say pizza?"

"That's what I told Blister."

"How about Thai instead?"

"He'll likely go along with that."

"Why do they call him Blister, anyway?"

"It's a long story," he said.

"So tell me while I dust."

He did.

Marlene had joined them, and the movie was nearing its climax. The heroine was scrambling through her lab, dumping liquid chemicals onto the floor, *splash,* overturning upright racks—in general creating a ruckus. "Why's she doing all that?" Leontine asked.

"You'll see in a minute," Connor answered.

The monster—roughly one-third lizard, two-fifths beetle, and a modicum of human, never mind how—was stegosaurus-sized, ill of temper, and currently in pursuit of the heroine, who had abandoned her dumping of flammables to pick up a small container of something unidentifiable.

"What's in the can?" said Marlene.

Connor, tongue firmly in cheek, said, "She's going to spray him with an insecticide."

Blister McGraw quipped, "That'll kill half of him."

Even Marlene laughed at that.

After the movie, the foursome played rummy for an hour. Snacks had proliferated, so Marlene offered—to the surprise of the two adults—to take the Thai residue out to the dumpster. "Just leave it," Leontine objected. "It's raining cats and canines. I'll trot it out in the morning."

"Let me slip into your raincoat," insisted Marlene, and the slender teenager did so. Adding a big floppy felt hat for good measure, she grabbed up two armfuls of paper bags and headed out the front door.

Junior Hughes, Junior, kept wiping condensation from the inside of the windshield, smudging the glass and drawing an objection from his partner, Piebald Sam Thrippin. "Junior, when you do that I gotta Windex the whole thing later. Just turn on the defrost, why don'tcha?" He stressed the first syllable in defrost.

"Gets too hot in here."

"Then run it through the AC, stoopit."

Junior looked hard at Piebald Sam. "Don't never call me stupid, 'less you want a teeth sandwich."

"The hell's a 'teeth sandwich'?" chuckled Piebald Sam. "What you mean's a knuckle sandwich. You're dumber'n a bowl of grout."

"Grout?"

"There she is!" hissed Piebald Sam.

And there she was.

The cascading rain pummeled Marlene's hat, *boppity-boppity,* as she skipped lightly toward the Dempsey Dumpster, avoiding the deeper puddles, the red mud seeping and clinging. *Better not slip,* she thought. *This coat would never come clean. I hate this frigging weather.*

Some jerk had closed the heavy sliding steel door, so she had to set down her parcels to grind it open. The grating *screee* assaulted her ears, masking the sound of an engine starting just across the slick dark road, in shadow, away from the lambency of the streetlight. As she picked up the damp bags, the car started to roll; as she tossed them in, the car gained speed; as she turned away from the opening, the car was almost on her, dark water sluicing from its all-weather radials. Marlene saw it too late, realized its intent too slowly, reacted like a deer caught in the headlights . . .

Until she screamed.

Then came the impact.

Connor was at the sink washing cups when he heard a scream that was abruptly stifled by a horrendous crash. Then the gunning of a car engine accompanied by severe gravel-grinding protestations from its tires as the automobile reversed itself, skidded to a halt, then changed course again, engine racing.

CRASH!

As the second impact came, Gibbs was going out the door.

"Where the hell is she?" yelled Junior Hughes, Junior.

"I don't see her! I think she ducked behind the dumpster!" Piebald Sam yelled back, pointing with half an index finger. "Lookit! Here comes that big sumbitch!"

"Yipe!" Junior exclaimed and rammed the shifter into reverse again, intent on a prudent—and *hasty*—retreat.

" 'Yipe'? What the hell's 'yipe'? Yell 'shit' or something, like a man!"

"Shit on *YOU*!" yelled Junior, toeing the throttle, whipping the wheel, slewing the front end around, gravel flying. In his rearview, he could see the big bastard closing in—pounding hard, feet sending up spray from the puddles—so he stuck the pedal to the firewall and held his breath until the Ford got a grip on the rain-slick surface and heaved itself forward, away from the threat and into the enveloping night.

"Oops!" said Junior Hughes, Junior, when they were safe.

" 'Oops'? The hell kinda comment is 'oops'? In case you didn't notice, that huge bastard was nearly up our ass when you finally got this thing straightened out and—"

"Where do you get off ragging *me*? I told *you* to drive, but no, you said it was *my* turn . . ."

And so it went until they abandoned their car in Durham and went to get stoned behind a Winn-Dixie.

Chapter 20

"Ohhh, THAT'S GONNA LEAVE SUCH A *BRUISE*!" Marlene lamented, her shapely but slender hip bared for Connor to examine. "That cocksucker!"

"There were two of them."

"Those cocksuckers!"

"That's better." Gibbs patted the injured area.

"Ouch, that hurts!" came the protest.

"You're lucky it does."

"Yeah? How?"

"You could be dead, Marlene. As in squashed. Look like strawberry marmalade."

"Or grape jam." She winced. "Why am I joking? This ain't funny."

"No, it isn't. But joking's better than crying."

"How about cussing?"

"Cussing is good."

"THOSE COCKSUCKERS!" they yelled together, then broke up laughing.

Leontine, returning from her 911 call, said, "You two think this is funny?"

"Better than crying," Marlene quoted, pulling up her jeans.

Leontine looked pointedly at Connor. "Did you enjoy the view?"

"Seen better."

"Only in your dreams, old man." Marlene slugged Connor's big arm, then sat uncomfortably on the couch, favoring the damaged cheek.

Connor asked, "How did they miss you?" just as Blister came in carrying the bare-bottomed baby, a soiled wipe in one hand. "This go in the toilet, or what?" the boy asked, nose wrinkled involuntarily.

"Come with me," snapped Leontine.

"Don't take me long to duck around a dumpster," Marlene explained to Gibbs. "But then again, if I'm so fast, how come this bruise, right?"

"So the car hit you, you didn't fall, or bump into something?"

"Damn right it hit me, and knocked me a loop. The other side of my butt's prob'ly got gravels in it."

Gibbs grinned again; he couldn't help but like this girl. She had extra helpings of spunk. "So you're okay?" he said.

"I reckon I'll live."

"Then I can make a phone call?"

"I don't need no nursemaid. Go make your old phone call."

So he did.

The first cop on the scene was a gent named Gentry, lean and swarthy and lisp-prone. He spoke with Marlene first, listening attentively and making notes in a little black spiral notebook as they sat on the couch. He then called FI to put out an APB on the car. As he hung up the phone, a second officer arrived.

"SI on the way?" asked Gentry.

"Who knows? They got the call the same time we did," responded the second cop, a freckle-faced blond who looked like a short Opie.

"Anybody want coffee?" queried Leontine from the kitchen, pot in hand. Both officers accepted her offer.

"Sorry, no doughnuts," lamented Gibbs.

"Ha-ha," Gentry said.

"Pretty lame," agreed Opie.

Then, while Gentry finished with Marlene, Opie questioned Connor. "How many people in the car?"

"Two," from Connor.

"Descriptions?"

"Males, not big. The one on the passenger side was pretty thin, in fact. Driver had on a navy ball cap."

"Race?"

"Human."

The cop looked up from his report.

"It was dark," Connor elaborated, "and raining. And half my attention was on Marlene."

The cop nodded. "Too dark to make the plate?"

"Georgia, 2D-44ZXL."

"You sure?"

"They drove under the streetlight making their getaway."

"Getaway. Right. What kind of car?"

"Ford LTD. Black, or possibly very dark blue. I'd vote for black."

"Any identifiable blemishes?"

Connor looked at Blister over in the corner rocking the baby, now asleep. Blister looked back and grinned pleasantly.

"The driver had a zit on his forehead," Gibbs offered. Blister was still grinning. Grinning and rocking.

"I meant the car, and you know it. Why're you busting my balls?" said Opie.

"Instinct and aversion."

"What?"

"Never mind. Any more questions?"

"Probably later." The cop turned to his partner, still interviewing Marlene. "You call the car in to FI?" he said.

The partner nodded without taking his attention off the girl.

"Plate, too?"

Nod.

Outside a van drove up. Opie looked out the kitchen window. "There's SI," he said, and stood, drained his cup, hitched his belt, put on his hat, and walked out the front door.

"You want to go to the hospital?" the swarthy cop was asking Marlene as Opie made his exit. "Get that hip looked at?"

Marlene, looking directly into Connor's eyes, said, "It's been looked at. Closely."

The cop swiveled his head toward Connor to glower.

Well, well, well, thought Gibbs. *He's smitten. And she knows it.* He winked at Marlene. She tossed it back. The cop was nonplussed, so he closed the little black notebook and his Bic repaired to a pocket. "That about does it," he said. "If you need us, don't hesitate to call." He stood, hitched his belt, put on his hat, gave Connor a scowl, and walked out the front door, saying "Thanks for the coffee" as he went.

When he was gone, Leontine shook her head at Gibbs. "You have scant respect for the police."

"It shows?" he said.

And then Holmes Crenshaw arrived.

"Tell me about it," said Crenshaw after settling into a chair with a mug of java.

Connor did—the short, succinct version.

"Helms, you think?" said Holmes at the conclusion.

"I think."

"Why Marlene?"

"Look at her."

Holmes did, as she sat next to Leontine on the couch. The resemblance was startling. "Right," said the lawyer.

"And remember, she was wearing a raincoat and a big floppy hat," Gibbs reminded.

"And it was dark and rainy out," added Holmes.

Gibbs nodded.

"We'll need to go speak with old Gantt. But not at his house," Holmes said.

"Why not?" asked Leontine.

"Heavily guarded. Without some kind of legal document, like a warrant, we'd have to fight our way in, through people and dogs. The man is, shall we say, inhospitable," from Gibbs.

"Well, maybe he'll meet you somewhere," suggested Blister.

Connor didn't respond right away. When he did, he just said, "He'll meet with me all right."

Crenshaw, not liking the tone of Connor's voice, sighed.

Chapter 21

"IT'S BEEN A WHILE, MY MAN," ALLOWED BRAXton Chiles, extending a long-fingered hand. Despite somewhat resembling Woody Allen, Chiles was one of the deadliest men Connor Gibbs had ever known. And one of the smelliest. Chiles disdained baths for reasons only he could explain, but never did. To anyone. Connor was careful to stand upwind.

"You've gained a little weight, Mr. Chiles," from Gibbs.

"Thank you for noticing. Yesterday I tipped the beam at 121 pounds."

"Lots of bench presses and bent rows?" Connor queried.

"Squats. My trainer preaches squat, squat, squat, if you want to pick up body weight."

"Why the sudden interest in physical culture?"

Chiles blushed through his scruffy goatee.

Gibbs was taken aback. Grinning, he said, "Really?"

Chiles blushed even deeper.

"It must be pretty serious."

Chiles nodded.

"That's great. Do I know her?"

Chiles shook his thick mop of hair. "I doubt it. She's from Paraguay."

"Nuptials in the offing?"

"Maybe," said Chiles, then segued, "What can I do for you?" Pleasantries over.

"I want a meet with Gantt Helms."

"No you don't. I hear he's angry at you."

"I'll risk it."

"Did you call him? He's in the book."

Gibbs shook his head. "I'll give you a deuce to set it up. As go between. No allegiance to either side."

"Make it four. Gantt figures if you aren't for him, you're against him."

Connor forked over four hundred-dollar bills.

Chiles said, "This buys you one phone call. Whether he shows is up to him."

"I understand."

"One thing. I'll try to arrange the meet off his turf, but he'll have Bingo with him, no question."

"Dog?"

Chiles nodded. "Helms is a dog man."

"Who's Bingo?"

"One bad freaking Alsatian."

"Thanks for the tip."

"I never gave it to you."

"Of course."

And they parted company.

Holmes Crenshaw was holding a dropper to his mouth. From it emitted a pale liquid, one drop, then another, onto his tongue. "What," said Connor Gibbs, "are you taking?"

"Flower power."

"I beg your pardon?"

"Little dab of snapdragon, to soothe. If you and I are going to toe up with that schmuck and his toothy Shetland pony, I'll need to keep a civil tongue in my beak," Crenshaw asserted. "Otherwise, we might get et."

"Snapdragon?"

"As in 'essence of.' Had a cup of chamomile tea ten minutes ago. Shortly, I'll be all mellowed out."

"You don't need to be mellow. You're not going."

"Like hell I'm not."

Leontine, on the couch with Jared, cooing and clucking, said, "Going where?"

The men ignored her.

Holmes said, "There is no way, *no* way, I'm letting you—"

"Holmie. Gantt has ratcheted the game up a notch. Who's going to look out for her?" He aimed a look at Leontine.

"Going where?" she said.

"I'll call Braxton."

"Can't. He's setting this up for me."

"Going where!" Leontine shouted.

Holmes said, "To have a prayerful discussion with Mr. Helms."

"Oh, no," from a perturbed Leontine Chevalier, "not without help, you aren't." She got up from the sofa, placed the baby in his crib, joined the men in the kitchen.

"Don't need help," Gibbs stated. Removing gauze from a large box on the counter, he methodically began to wrap his left forearm, around and around, layer after layer, as the others watched.

Leontine was mystified. "What are you doing that for?"

"Tennis elbow," Gibbs quipped.

Holmes Crenshaw asked, "What if he goes for the groin?"

"I'll improvise."

"What if *who* goes for the groin?" Leontine asked, the telltale vertical furrow creasing her forehead.

"What if he has two along?" from Holmes.

"He won't," Connor disagreed. "Wouldn't be able to control two, not in any setting Chiles will pick."

"Two *what*?" said Leontine.

"How about if he brings along a few sluggers?"

"Same answer. Chiles will put us in a highly visible, very public place. Gantt's only shot is to sic a pooch on me. He might be able to defend that, even should witnesses abound. Just say the dog went gaga at the sight of my ugly mug."

"This isn't funny," Holmes said.

"What dog?" from Ms. Chevalier.

"Of course it isn't," Connor agreed with his friend. "That's why I'm doing this." He finished wrapping, securing the gauze, and slipped his thickened arm carefully into the sleeve of a heavy winter coat. Stepping away from the other two, he moved his left arm up, down, across, then said, "Detectable?"

"Not very," Crenshaw assessed.

"Would you two please tell me what's going on?" Leontine said.

"No," the men said together, just as the phone rang.

Connor jerked up the receiver. "Chevalier residence."

Then he mostly listened.

"I've got a Kahr 9mm in the glove compartment," Holmes insisted.

"No thanks."

"Connor."

"Holmes."

Crenshaw sighed. "Call me."

"Soon as it's over."

"Where do you want the flowers sent?"

"To Gantt's house."

That drew a laugh, anyway.

A small, nervous one.

Holmes was worried about his friend.

As Connor Gibbs motored toward the freeway, he punched numbers on his digital phone.

"Hello," came the response.

"Peiffer Park," said Gibbs. "One-fifteen. Braxton's instructions were for no one but Gantt to be there, but I expect a few kibitzers."

"I'll be on 'em like a fly on cheesecake. More than two, though, spread out, could be a problem. You have a contingency plan?"

"The National Guard."

Throaty laughter from the other end, amid the static. "You take care of the arm?"

"It's so stiff I can scarcely move it."

A pause then. "You're sure about this?"

"I learned the move in Korea ten years ago. I've done it before, for real, not in training. It's no fun, but I can handle it."

"You're certainly strong enough. You nervous?"

"No."

"How come?"

"Zen."

Snort of derision. "Well, don't let Zen bite you in the ass."

And they rang off.

Chapter 22

COREY E. PEIFFER PARK (NAMED FOR A RELA-
tively obscure submariner who invented something even
more obscure for use on diesel-powered submersible ships
during the First World War, and which was produced in a
factory originally on the site) was situated centrally in Wendover and drew crowds year round. There were tennis courts,
a ball diamond, a tarmacked basketball court, a pool, fishing
ponds, an ornate gazebo, lots of trees and grass, and mud
when it rained or after a fresh snow. Some of it squished underfoot as Connor trudged to the bleachers adjacent to the
baseball field. As he started up into the stands, a whistle
stopped him. Turning his head to engage the whistler, Gibbs
saw Gantt Helms step clear of the visitors' dugout, alone except for the largest Alsatian Gibbs had ever seen—at least
150 pounds of hair and teeth and scar tissue. Well, maybe
not much scar tissue; dogs that will attack humans are seldom inclined to fight one another. With a fat hand, Helms
motioned a "come hither" to Connor. Connor went, most of
the way.

Not all.

Distance can be a comforting thing sometimes.

Right then, for instance.

Stopping thirty feet away, Gibbs stared into Gantt's eyes.

"Careful about the scary fucking looks. Bingo don't like 'em," grunted Helms.

Connor stared some more.

"You hear what I said?"

"Yeah, I heard. And I don't give a rat's ass what Bingo likes," Connor explained.

Gantt's eyes glittered with amusement. "No shit? Maybe we can modify that view, me and old Bingo."

"I came to talk, Helms. That's all. Talk. But let's come to an understanding before we begin. If you turn that dog loose on me, I'll kill it."

The glitter turned harsh, piercing. "Big words, even for such a big man. But Bingo here don't care how big you are. Just be more for him to chew on."

Gibbs shrugged. "I warned you."

"So noted," Helms said. "Now what's up?"

"Lay off Leontine Chevalier."

"Hell, she's the one threatened me."

"Do you blame her?"

Helms glanced back at the dugout, then reached a pudgy hand under his sweater to scratch an itch. "No, I don't blame her, but I still can't let her get away with it. Makes me look bad to my friends."

"A man like you has no friends, but no matter, it would be best for you to just let this go. It's more than you can handle."

Helms fixed Connor's eyes again. "Don't go telling me what to do, Gibbs. It ain't healthy. Now, here's the way it's gonna play, so listen up. You drop that bimbo off at my place. She and I'll have a little chat. She'll get her come-uppance, I'll get the egg off my face she put there with that silly fucking TV interview, and everybody'll come away a winner, 'cept maybe her. I'll even leave some of that snatch intact, for you to poke when I bring her sorry ass back. How's that suit you, boy?"

Gibbs returned the look for perhaps thirty seconds, then said, voice hollow, "Are we going to the wall on this?"

"You don't even want to think about taking me on, you fucking gorilla!" Helms spat onto the snow, a yellow wad of phlegm.

"Because if we do, you're going to lose," Gibbs finished calmly.

And Helms lost it. "BINGO!" he screeched, pointing.

Bingo leaped as if from a cannon . . .

. . . three, four strides, long legs extended, and then launched his taunt, muscular body . . .

Straight for Connor's throat.

Gibbs stood his ground and then—with the dog's gaping muzzle barely inches from his neck—brought up his encased forearm to block the attack.

Bingo latched onto the arm with incredible force, bared canines sinking almost to the bone, and the dog's careening body slammed into Gibbs, forcing the man back a step as his right arm was coming up, around, *behind* Bingo's head, to the base of the dog's skull, just behind the ears, where the arm then locked rigidly into place, to pull the animal forward, holding it off the ground, against the man's barrel chest . . .

. . . As the padded left arm—into which the dreaded teeth were still sunk—came up and over, toward the restrictive right arm, the move unexpected, lightning quick, unbelievably powerful . . .

It snapped Bingo's head back, breaking the dog's neck like a stick.

The magnificent animal moved very little after it fell to the ground.

Benella Mae Sweet sloshed through the slush, dressed in red skin-tight, knee-length shorts, a Green Bay jersey, black

Nikes, and a scarlet headband to control errant locks. Looks flashed her way as she ran. They always did. She was impervious. And intent. She could see Connor and Helms in the distance, over at the edge of the infield with a dog as big as a mule, but no one else did she espy. Which was her job; watching, covering her man's backside. She felt like Hillary Clinton.

In the parking lot nearby, a van sat open-doored. Odd. It was 37 degrees and cloudy. She veered. As she drew nearer to the van, she glanced over at Connor in time to see the Alsatian make its move, and in seconds meet its demise. She shook her head once, at the waste, just as a long slim black barrel protruded from the van's open rear door. The barrel was aimed in Connor's direction. She deflected the gun barrel just in time, causing it to fire into the ground, sending up a geyser of mud, then swung her magnificent body into the bowels of the truck. Two men there, one holding a long slim black rifle. She grabbed the barrel of the gun and pointed it at the second man, who yelped and dove for the front seat just as the rifle fired again, its bullet digging entrails from the seatback and going on to smash the windshield. Cracking the shooter on the jaw twice very hard with her right elbow softened his resolve to hold onto his weapon. He fell into a heap at her feet. The second man was now on the floor in the front, covering his head with both arms.

"You," barked Benella.

No response, except for much cowering and quivering.

"If I have to drag my lengthy body up there to fetch you, one of us is going to be unhappy about it."

The man peeked out from under his arms. "You talking to me?"

"Well, this one's beyond hearing," she said, prodding the shooter with a Nike.

The second man climbed into the back with Bennie. She suggested that they quit the truck, and once on the tarmack she asked, "You the Gantt Helms contingent?"

"What's a contingent?"

Bennie shook her golden head in exasperation. "You with Helms?"

"Yeah."

"What's your name?"

"Junior."

"Junior what?"

"Junior Hughes, Junior."

She shook her head again. "Anyone else around?"

"Just Gantt's brother, down in the dugout."

"So you were going to stand by and let that lump of weasel sperm in the van shoot my sugar pie?"

"That's what Gantt tolt us to do. Back up Sherm."

"You aren't much as backup," Benella said, and front-kicked the man in the gonads. Down he went, to moan and clutch. "Not much on stoicism, either," Bennie said contemptuously, then tossed the long slim black rifle into a trash barrel—after unloading it, of course—and went to check on Connor.

Gantt Helms's reaction to the death of Bingo was instantaneous and unequivocal: He went berserk. Digging at his waistband, he produced a small semi-automatic pistol and was leveling it when Gibbs hit him an overhand right that sat the plump fellow in the snow. Suddenly, Sherman was beside his brother, striving to calm. "Whoa, pal. Folks're watching. There's a time and a place, and this ain't neither," he said.

The younger Helms was having none of it; up came the little pistol again. This time Connor grabbed the gun, jerked it loose from the fat, clammy grasp, and rang the man's chimes with a palm to the ear. "OUCH!" screamed Gantt Helms, falling heavily to one side. When Sherman tried to retaliate on his sibling's behalf, Gibbs hit him with a left hook that crossed his eyes, then walked away leaving the Helmses in a pain-racked pile.

• • •

Bennie caught up with Connor near first base. "Howdy, sailor," she sang.

"You're in a fine mood. You must have kicked someone's derrière."

"Two someones, in fact." She took his arm in hers. "Why're you so grumpy? The dog?"

He nodded.

"Did Helms sic it on you?"

He nodded again.

"Well, there you go. Attack dogs can be hard to reason with, especially in mid-attack."

"I know."

"Still hurts though, right?"

Nod.

She squeezed his arm. "You're the gentlest man I ever met, and still people make you do these things."

His blue eyes glistened. "Not the dog's fault. Could have been Zepper."

"No, you raised Zepper. Gantt Helms made that dog what it was. You know that, right?"

Nod.

"Sugar pie?"

He looked into her eyes as they walked.

"Learn to live with things like this, or choose another avocation."

He nodded one last time.

"I'll make you whole again, later," she promised.

He smiled grimly. "You always do."

"And always will."

"Always?"

"Yes. We're one heart, you know?"

He knew.

Chapter 23

Slide Websen said to "Pepper" Jenesais-Quoi, "Them Presas got potential?" Pepper was unloading sacks of dog food from the rear of a Nissan four-wheel-drive wagon.

"All dogs have potential. Fewer trainers," Pepper said.

"They'll make good fighters, then?"

"Time will tell."

"Gantt's looking to recoup his outlay on those. They cost him a shitload of cash."

Pepperoy shrugged. "We shall see."

"That's not what Gantt wants to hear."

Pepper shrugged again. "I train fighting dogs, I am not a counselor."

"Gantt might not appreciate the attitude."

Pepper looked up at Websen. "I am working. Is there anything else?"

"Jewel is going against the Russkie tomorrow."

Pepper straightened. "The Ovcharka?"

"Yeah. Will she win?"

Pepper bent back to his task. "Yes."

"You're sure? That's one hellacious hairball. Thirty inches high, 140 pounds, mean as a sackful of rattlers. Damn near uncontrollable is what I hear."

"Jewel will win."

"I got your personal guarantee on that?"

"Call it a prediction."

"'Cause Gantt is pretty upset over Bingo, and if—"

Pepper straightened again after tossing another feed bag onto the pallet behind him. "What about Bingo?"

"You ain't heard? Some bastard killed him."

"How?"

"With his bare fucking hands, is what I was told."

Pepper wiped his brow, took in the ominous sky. "More snow coming," he said, then grabbed another bag of feed. "Must have been some man."

"Bigger than Little Boy is the way I get it. Taller at least."

"Little Boy will not be pleased. He nursed that dog along like family."

"Don't I know it. I suspect Gantt might send Little Boy down to talk with this dog-killing son of a bitch."

Pepperoy said, "Perhaps."

"Keep us posted on them Presas."

Pepper's nod ended the conversation.

Little Boy was lying on the floor in front of a Christmas tree (Scotch pine) that he had recently decorated, listening to Ethan James on CD. James was playing a French bourbonnis hurdy-gurdy in D, loudly, when Slide Websen slid in the door.

"Can you turn that down?" Websen shouted.

"No. But you can," returned Little Boy.

Slide did so. Then sat on an ottoman. Stroked his cleft chin. Pretended to admire the decorations.

"What do you want?" asked the prostrate Little Boy.

Sarcastically, "A mulled cider."

"Got some eggnog in the fridge, if it hasn't turned. Put some brandy in it if you want."

"What's baking?" from Slide Websen, sniffing the air.

"Fairings."

"What?"

"You'd say gingerbread."

"Then why'd you call it fairings?"

"In Europe, gingerbread was a favorite at fairgrounds. In fact, fairs were often referred to as 'gingerbread fairs.' "

"I get it."

"There was once a tradition in England for unmarried ladies to eat gingerbread 'husbands' at the fair, to aid in their search for a real one."

Websen chuckled. "Bet Gloria Steinem'd love that."

"It'll be ready in about eight minutes. Made up some lemon sauce for the topping."

"What's with baking? You a little light on your feet?"

Little Boy turned his head to look at Websen.

"Hey, just kidding."

"My mama taught me to bake. When I was little and she was at work in the evening, I'd bake bread for the table. Word got around, and soon I was selling more than I could bake. It helped a lot. Mama didn't make much at the brewery."

"Where was your dad?"

Little Boy's face clouded over, and he looked back at the tree. "What do you want, Slide?"

"You hear about Bingo?"

Eyes shifting back to Websen, "What about him?"

Websen told.

Immediately after the recounting, Little Boy seemed to levitate; one moment he was supine, the next vertical. No effort seemed to have been expended.

Man, can he move, especially for a big guy, thought Websen, as Little Boy picked up the phone and dialed.

• • •

Gantt Helms was feeding his fat face and brooding; he missed Bingo. Sherman was stabbing at a tooth with a pick and belching softly. The two were otherwise alone.

"Fight's tomorrow," said Sherman.

"I know when the fucking fight is," around a forkful of chocolate layer cake.

"You plan to lay off any bets?"

"Hell no. Carry the load."

"What if . . . ?" Sherman's thought was interrupted; the phone was ringing. He got up to answer it.

"Little Boy," he said to Gantt, hand covering the receiver.

Gantt waved it off. "Tell him I'll get back to him. I ain't in the mood."

Sherman relayed the message, then again covered the mouthpiece. "He's sort of insistent."

"Ask him who the fuck pays who!" shouted Helms.

Sherman did so, then hung up. Back at the table he said, "Why not bring Little Boy in on this? Let him take care of Gibbs?"

"I need Little Boy right where he is. The operation would go to hell without him up there. We'll take care of Gibbs ourselves. He's big, but he can't turn a bullet."

"Those two yesterday might not agree."

Gantt chewed the last of his cake before speaking. "Hell, it was Gibbs's fucking girlfriend did that. Who knew? I'll need to talk to them boys, by the way."

"They know, and they're petrified."

"Musta heard about Mo."

"I reckon."

"Put Iggy on Gibbs right now. Sanction the cocksucker."

"Now, Gantt—"

"Don't 'Now Gantt' me, Sherm. Put Iggy on Gibbs *right fucking now*!"

Sherman made the call.

• • •

"Well damn, Connor," said Braxton Chiles.

Gibbs, phone to his ear, said nothing.

Which spoke volumes to Chiles.

"I feel pretty bad about this," from Braxton.

"No one made me go."

"I hear it was propitious that Benella went along."

"Um-hm."

"I also hear that Iggy Cremins has been given carte blanche to whack you."

"Who?"

"The slender gent you danced with at the trailer park."

"What about the other one?"

"Now deceased. Lost his voice, and most of his throat with it."

Connor digested that. "Helms must be a pretty strict disciplinarian."

"I gather," Chiles agreed.

"Thanks for the word, Mr. Chiles."

"I've been considering this neutrality pact we have, and I may abandon it. I don't like how this is shaping up, and I especially don't like you having to rely on the lovely Ms. Sweet to cover your flank."

"She can manage. And I have Holmes Crenshaw."

"Right. And if it gets sticky, who faces disbarment?"

"That's primarily why he wasn't with me at the park."

"So who else you got?"

"Rex Jobie might help out."

Chiles guffawed at that. "I'm conscripting myself, Connor. But I'll bill you big time if I have to make a hit."

"Like you did with Wacky Mavens?"

Chiles made a sound. "Wacky needed whacking."

"You still have the tie?"

Chiles grinned, though Gibbs couldn't see it. But he could hear it in his voice. "You bet. That tie's gotten me laid at least thrice that I know of."

"Thrice?"

"Iggy may not be tough physically, except with a kosh, but he's poison mean. So I'm on your team, Connor, right now as a bloodhound. I'll be in touch." He hung up.

"Who was that?" Leontine asked when Connor came over to sit beside her.

"Doc Holliday."

"Don't you ever give a straight answer?"

Gibbs said nothing.

Leontine shook her head and turned back to the TV.

Chapter 24

Connor Gibbs knew Gantt Helms would shift into high gear now. Retribution time. In fact, Gibbs had planned it that way. A rapid conclusion to something like this was always preferable. What he didn't know was exactly what Leontine Chevalier was up to. He'd never bought her "please keep me from shooting the bastard" line, though it was obvious the woman needed help. So he'd agreed. It was, after all, what he did in life—help people.

"What do you do about money?" she had once asked him.

"Let my accountant take care of it," he'd answered.

"Where does it come from?" she'd pried.

"My income?"

"Yes."

"Nosey aren't we?" he'd picked.

"Just curious."

"You know that Holiday Inn they just built at the airport?"

"Yep."

"I owned the land."

"How many acres?"

"I sold them thirty."

"You owned more?"

"It used to belong to my granddaddy. He farmed it for fifty years."

"How much do you still own?"

"Of that parcel?"

"You have others?"

"During the Depression, my granddaddy bought a lot of land."

"So, how much?" she'd pressed.

"Of the airport tract, only twenty acres left, give or take."

"You sold some off to somebody else?"

"You remember that FedEx runway they built three years ago?"

She'd whistled through her front teeth. "You're kidding. Did you get a lot for it?"

"Not as much as Holiday Inn paid me, at least not per acre."

"Then you're rich."

"Donnie Trump occasionally borrows money from me."

She'd smiled at that. "*Donnie* Trump?"

"We're pals."

"Does he call you Connie?"

"No, that's my sister."

"You have a sister?"

"I can if I want to," he'd said, and gone on to other things.

Currently, he was packing his duffle, and Leontine was in her room packing hers and Jared's. She yelled down the hall: "I hate to go off and leave the trailer, what with it decorated and all."

"My house is spruced up, too."

"Don't I know. I went there with you, remember? It's just that, well, this old place has never looked so good. Money was always tight for me and Sam."

And then she appeared in the doorway to Connor's room, Jared in one arm, a suitcase in the other, her hair drawn back in a ponytail. "I'm ready," she announced.

"And I," he announced right back.

So they left.

"Tell me again why this move," Leontine said. Jared was asleep in a car seat in the back of Connor's van.

"I figure our pal Gantt will pull out all the stops, now, and Braxton Chiles pretty much confirms it."

"Who?"

"An acquaintance of mine, with his ear to the underground rail. Anyway, my house is easier to defend than your place. Plus we've moved the playing field, which should cut down on collateral damage."

"On what?"

"Hurt bystanders. Like Marlene."

"Oh. Right."

Jared's little face, softly in repose, twitched when Gibbs hit a pothole. "Oops," said Connor, noting in the mirror. "Sorry, little guy. Tried to miss it."

Jared didn't respond.

"Probably dreaming of stewed spinach," said Gibbs.

"His favorite," Leontine chuckled.

And the phone rang.

"Quixote, Inc.," Connor said into it.

"What a ridiculous name." It was Vera McGraw, Blister's aunt.

"What can I do for you, Vera?"

"Cody asked to spend Christmas with you."

"You still won't call him Blister, will you?"

"His name is Cody. Did you tell him he could?"

"Told him it was up to you."

"If he's with you, who's with me on Christmas?"

"That's why I told him to check with you. Figured you might have other plans."

"None of the Sizemores have invited him."

"Maybe since Tate died right after Thanksgiving, their mood is somber."

"Maybe it's because they're a bunch of redneck deviants."

"Maybe you should work on your Christmas spirit."

"Maybe I'll keep Cody here with me."

"I assumed you would."

"And you put the onus on me to tell him."

"Well, I certainly have no objection to his staying."

"What about the Chevalier woman?"

"What about her?"

"Will she be there?"

"Unless I manage to resolve her situation before then."

"What kind of *woman*," oozing scorn, "would have a man come live with her she doesn't even know?"

"One who is in danger. Don't oppugn Ms. Chevalier, Vera. You don't know her."

"Cody will stay with me on Christmas," Vera breathed and hung up.

As Gibbs put down his digital, Leontine said, "Oppugn?"

" 'Call into question.' "

"Oppugn," she repeated to herself. "How many words do you know?"

"Eleven," he said and dodged a pothole. Jared's face stayed smooth.

Connor put Leontine in the bedroom next to his, upper floor, and reintroduced her to Oreo. "Feel free to plunder the refrigerator," he instructed and went to fetch the mail.

In the stack, a letter from Cameron, out in California. He felt a tug as he read:

Dear Daddy,

Mom and I just got back from this town called Sebastopol, where there's this place called Georgetown run by an old man who was in Gone with the wind. Did you ever see it? Some guy named Clark Gables was in it. Anyway they had this carriage from the movie, and some sword used by Earl Flin in this other movie, and President Reagon's coat. And this rope used by Will Rogers, who I guess is Roy Rogers brother. Everything was in this old timey house with a wagon wheel and an old coke machine on the porch, and tin signs. Neato.

I'm doing Intermezzo and Toccatina at the Christmas recital. Mrs. Kirk says my fingers are coming right along, haha. School's all As, well one B, in social studies, yuk, but our basketball team is really laying them low. I've played every game, but I don't score all that many goals. Mom says I play good defense, but to work on my shots. So I spend a few minutes outside the garage every day, playing horse by myself. This neighborhood is ALL GIRLS. Double YUK!

Well, mom says I need to do my homework, not spend all day writing to you, so I better go. I love you.

Your son,
Cameron

Gibbs carefully refolded the letter and put it in his desk, with the few others he'd received since . . . then. He turned away, trudged up the stairs, and lay on his bed for fifteen minutes, his heart aching.

Chapter 25

DOWN A LONG AND WINDING ROAD NEAR THE
border of Georgia and South Carolina, between Tallulah
Falls and Clarkesville, squats a low cinderblock building
surrounded by forest, hill, and combe. The building is old
and vine-covered, morose, as if ashamed of itself and its
purpose, surrounded by a graveled lot that on one weekend
per month contains a multitude of vehicles, not all pickup
trucks with gunracks in the rear window. Often there are
Lexus coupes, an occasional Ferrari, a red Porsche, Cadil-
lacs galore, a Mercedes. Inside, the array of humanity is as
eclectic as their means of conveyance, not all inbred low-
brow low-lifes, but respected lawyers, a doctor or two, an ar-
chitect, several CEO's, and a minister, nondenominational.
The mood is anticipatory, profane, raucously licentious,
marked by cupidity; Aunt Bee won't be found in this crowd.

In the center of the building is a cement pit, not especially
large but surrounded by elevated seating as in a gymnasium,
and a low wall—to keep combatants from running amuck
amid the patrons. The pit bottom contains a drain, to allow
the flushing of fecal matter, hair, and blood.

Mostly blood.

This gathering likes blood.

It stirs theirs. Makes wallets fairly leap from pockets.

Marvin, the former marine dog handler, was in one corner talking to Pepper, the Canadian dog trainer. "Those Presas working out?" asked Marvin.

Pepper said, "Too soon to tell. They're going to be large, perhaps 120 pounds. Presas are like American bulldogs, furious fighters at first, but they tire quickly."

"The Jewel doesn't. Though her weight's down some."

Pepper swung his head in concern. "Why?"

"Hell, I don't know. Some bad feed, or a bug. She had a bout with diarrhea a couple weeks ago, but she's in the pink now. Dropped maybe four–five pounds. She weighed in at 163."

"And the Ovcharka?"

"One-forty-one. Big bastard. I hear that pissweed Helstrom from Atlanta brought a Korean Jindo to go against Rocky's pit bull."

"Jindo?"

"Looks like an Akita. They say the dog's built a rep down South, though I don't know what he's fought," from Marvin. A tall man in bib overalls bumped into him while ferrying hot dogs to a short man in a suit. Marvin glared at them. They both ignored him.

Marvin said, "Did you hear about that pit out west going into the ring with a young tiger?"

"A tiger, *sacre bleu.*"

The crowd was beginning to heat up; fight number four was imminent, and the bets were flying.

"An adolescent cat, maybe 150 pounds," Marvin continued. "The pit didn't weigh sixty."

"And?"

"The tiger spent a lot of time on its back, of course, but the pit sensed the danger from the claws and circled. In the end, the tiger lost." Marvin shook his head. "Pits give all they got."

"Often they will defeat a Tosa-Inu that outweighs them four to one, then die afterward," Pepper agreed.

"All heart."

"Yes. Like the Jewel."

"I never dealt with a Tosa-Fila cross before, but she seems to have all the good stuff. Size, ferocity, stamina, and not an ounce of quit."

"But the Russkie is savage," worried Pepper. "And has much coat for her to bite through. And it is said to be ver' quick."

"The Ovcharka? You're right about all that, but this dog's no Russkie. A south Russian or Caucasian Ovcharka wouldn't last three minutes with Jewel. This is a Middle Asian dog."

Pepper turned his head again. "Is that bad?"

"It ain't good."

Now Pepper was really worried.

Gantt Helms and Little Boy had front-row seating. Around them the crowd surged and ebbed and shouted itself hoarse as an Argentine Dogo was being pummeled by a mastiff/Staffordshire terrier crossbreed. Gantt was saying, "Fucking Dogo's are hunting dogs, pack runners. Shouldn't even be in the ring with that other bastard."

Fur was flying, the din incredible amid shouting and cursing and vocal canine bloodlust. The mastiff mix was having a fine time. Less so the Argentine.

"Got the cars painted, renumbered, shipped to Kansas City," intoned Little Boy, uninterested in the deadly tableau in progress.

"GO IN LOW, YOU STUPID MUTT!" Gantt shouted. "Lookit that, dumb fuck. I got three bills on him. How about the grass?"

"Websen took a load to Richmond last night. No more for a while."

Gantt nodded. "You got the—GET UP, GET UP!" He jumped to his fat feet and pumped a fist, then sat heavily.

"You got the operation running smooth as a cue ball, I gotta admit. Since you took over, all I do is count the money." He laughed at that, then in an affected voice: "Count de Money, Count de Money. You see that Mel Brooks flick? *History of the World,* or something?"

"I don't go to movies."

"So what *do* you do all fucking night up there in the boonies, play choke the chicken? There sure as hell ain't no women worth poking, not that I ever seen. DID YOU SEE THAT MOVE!" Up again jumped Helms, jostling the man beside him, who tossed him a look and started to protest, then noticed the implacable Little Boy and quickly looked away.

Once Gantt was reseated, Little Boy said, "What happened to Bingo?"

Helms frowned. "Don't you worry about that. I got Iggy on it and a couple of others in the wings. You just take care of business like you been doing, and I'll do the same in my own backyard."

"Bingo meant something to me."

"Hell, boy, you think I didn't feel the same? That fucking dog stuck to me like shit on shoeleather, and covered my broad ass more than once. There was this one time in Cincinnati . . . well, never mind. Dog's dead, that's all. And the asshole who did it will root the day, I guarantee."

"Rue," said Little Boy.

"What?"

"Rue the day. Not root."

"What-the-fuck-ever. LOOKIT THAT!" The Dogo had lost an eye and was trying to get out of the ring, but the mastiff would have none of it, and the Argentine's owner was nowhere in sight.

In short order there was more blood to wash away.

The Jewel lay in her cage, waiting. Soon Master would come. Fighting did not really engage the dog; pleasing Master did, at least so far as anyone could tell. Fighting was her job. And killing.

She did it for Him.

The Middle Asian Ovcharka, whose name was Charon, took the adjective "high-strung" to new heights. He paced his cage, snapping at the occasional flea ensconced in its shaggy pelisse, and slavered from anticipation. Charon liked to fight, *lived* to fight.

And to kill.

"Fifteen grand on Charon," leered the lawyer from Myrtle Beach.

"Make it twenty-five," from Gantt Helms.

"Done," said the barrister. "The Jewel ready?"

"She's always ready," said Gantt Helms.

"Then let's get started."

Around the ring, onlookers accreted like drops of urine on a sullied urinal as Gantt Helms went to get the Jewel.

Master was coming. Jewel could smell him. Hear him. *Feel* him.

And then he was there.

It took two men to leash the Ovcharka, two to lead it to the pit, walking on opposing sides of the dog, two to hold it while the muzzle was being removed. Then they scattered as if a barnyard bull had been released.

Or something even more deadly.

Gantt Helms said, "Heel!" and the Jewel exited her cage to come to heel, left side rear.

The two of them proceeded to the arena alone, no leash.

Bystanders cleared a path. A wide one.

There was no need. The Jewel was under complete control.

And then Gantt stopped, bent down, lifted, heaved . . .
And Jewel was in the pit.

The Ovcharka came in fast and low and immediately, going for the throat. What it got was dewlap, and not much of that. The Jewel was too fast. And too strong. And too agile. Too determined. Too good.

And too incredibly, ferociously *intent*.

After five and a half minutes Gantt Helms yelled, "JEWEL," and the huge dog quit.

Charon, lying at her feet, was not dead.

Except in spirit.

He never fought again.

But the Jewel would.

Once.

Chapter 26

"HE'S WETTING THE BED."

Oh God. "Every night?"

"No, just twice since he's been here. But hey, dear sister-in-law," said LouAnne Ashley, "if two mean dogs had chewed on me, I'd pee myself too. And much more often."

LouAnne was thirty-something, had dark, short hair, Yankee brusqueness, clipped intonations, and a great, huge heart, as had her late brother. She worked for the state of New Jersey, but was currently on medical leave. Muscular arthritis, she said.

Leontine, munching a Frito, said into the phone, "Is he still in bed?" It was seven-fifteen in the morning.

"You bet. They were up late last night watching some Jackie Chan pic." The "they" included LouAnne's two boys, Edmund and Sack (an attenuation of Sackathorn, a family surname).

"Not too violent, I hope."

"Not as violent as getting chewed on by dogs, I'll guarantee."

"I meant—"

"He's fine, honey. Just fine. What's a few wet sheets. Oh, and neither of my boys know."

Whew. "Is he eating okay?"

"Like a baby bird, anything you put in his mouth."

"Can you have him call when he gets up?"

"Sure I can."

Leontine gave her new number, or rather Connor's number.

"You move?" from LouAnne, instantly suspicious.

"Temporarily."

"In with somebody?"

"Yes, but not like you think."

"How else is there?"

"I'll explain it all later."

"Okay. How's little Jared?"

"He's fine," from Leontine, crunching another Frito. "Getting too fat. Soon, I'll have to lug him around in a backpack."

That elicited a laugh. "Just like his daddy. Well, hon, it's your dime, but—"

"I know, we better hang up. Just remember to have Eddie call."

"Will do. Bye, now."

And half a bag of corn chips went south.

Connor came in from his run at five 'til eight, breath slightly ragged, but not wheezing. "How far did you run?" asked Leontine, a glass of juice in one hand. She handed it to him.

"Little over five miles."

"You're a pretty big guy to run that far. Sam couldn't have run a mile, and he played football all through high school."

"You have to stick with it. Legs are the first to go," Gibbs replied, heading down the hall.

"You want me to fix breakfast for you while you shower?"

"Yeah, if it'll keep you from climbing in with me."

She grinned at that. "No promises. Eggs?"

"That'll be fine."

"How many?"

"A half dozen, and pumpernickel toast if you don't mind, four or five pieces. The kudzu jelly is inside the door of the refrigerator."

"Hot tea?"

"Milk will be fine, thanks."

"So, what's on the agenda for today?" from Leontine.

"I need shearing."

"Do tell. I was beginning to be embarrassed being seen with such a shaggy brute."

"You want to tag along, or stay here?"

"It's not dangerous for me to be here alone for a few hours?"

"I can ask Richard Abernathy—"

"Here we come," she interrupted, scooping up Jared from where he lay on the floor as Gibbs skipped lightly up the stairs, no mean feat for a man weighing nearly 250 pounds.

"We're going out of town?" Leontine queried.

Gibbs nodded in response.

"Where to?" Leontine was sitting sideways in the front seat, holding a bottle for Jared to deplete. Jared, strapped into a child's seat in the back, was doing his part.

"Mount Airy," from Connor.

"That's fifty miles away."

Gibbs just steered.

"Isn't it?" Leontine pressed.

"More like thirty-eight."

"Why Mount Airy?"

"Lady named Rae cuts hair there."

"No one in Wendover cuts hair?"

"Not like Rae."

"She's good enough to drive forty miles one way?"

Gibbs nodded as, five cars back, Iggy Cremins trailed along in a hot Dodge.

• • •

"What's so special about this Mount Airy woman?"

"Don't call her that."

Leontine was returning Jared's diminished bottle to her tote bag. "Call her what?" she said absentmindedly.

" 'This Mount Airy woman.' Her name is Rae."

Leontine gave him her full attention. "Touchy, aren't we. You and Rae got a history?"

Gibbs glanced away from the road for a second. Just a brief, sideways look. Leontine, whatever else she was, wasn't stupid. And she needed this man. "I'm sorry. You're protective of your friends. It's a nice quality to have. Forget I said anything about . . . Rae."

Gibbs nodded and drifted onto the entrance ramp to Highway 52, heading north.

Iggy Cremins did likewise. Beside him on the seat was an Ithaca twelve-gauge autoloader, its barrel cut to eighteen inches so it could be fired one-handed. It was loaded with buckshot, magnum shells, lethal and loud. Gantt had promised fifty thousand for Connor Gibbs, and that skinny broad riding with him was worth another ten grand. The baby, Iggy would throw in for free, sort of a bonus. Iggy hated babies. "All they do is eat and shit and cry and vomick," he mumbled to himself, fairly grinning as he trundled along.

The good citizens of Mount Airy would speak of this day for years to come.

Not fondly.

A bare quarter mile ahead of Iggy Cremins, the Gibbs minivan pulled into a parking lot just past Wal-Mart. Gibbs left his motor idling and hoofed it into a small rectangular building featuring dark wood siding. Iggy motored past, hung a quick right at a signal light, drove into a Hardee's, and parked with an unobstructed view of Connor's car. In less than a minute, Gibbs returned and drove away.

Iggy did too.

• • •

"Well?" from Leontine Chevalier.

"Rae had a cancellation, so she went to the nursing center to see her mother, which she does every day. She isn't back yet."

"Didn't you have an appointment?"

"Can't get Rae to cut your hair if you don't. But we're early. I was hoping to catch her between cuts, sitting at her desk reading, but no luck. You want a snack?"

Leontine looked at her watch. "Like what?"

"Ice cream."

She shrugged thin shoulders. "Why not."

So they headed for the Bluebird Diner.

Now on West Pine, headed east, Connor Gibbs noticed a Dodge Intrepid in his rearview. The car was sort of a yellowish tan and contained but one occupant. He'd noticed it once while on 52, but had then lost sight of it. As they passed Weiner-Burger on their right, the Intrepid was three cars back, in the righthand lane. As they passed Olde Mill Music, the Dodge was directly aft. Just after Moody Service, they crossed South Main, swung left onto Renfro, then a left again at East Oak. The fulvous Intrepid, though not close, clung like tape. After a turn onto North Main, the Bluebird Diner was coming up on Connor's left. There was a parking slot in front of Pages Books and Magazines, but on impulse Gibbs passed it up.

"Why do you keep watching the mirror?" Leontine asked.

Gibbs said, "We have a tail," then snapped, *"Don't look!"*

Leontine stiffened like a sparrow spotting a cat.

Connor eased up to a stoplight diagonally across from the Mount Airy post office, stopping in the right lane, behind a Subaru wagon.

The Intrepid pulled up beside them.

And all hell broke loose.

• • •

Iggy poked the shotgun toward his passenger-side window, which he'd had the foresight to lower in anticipation of just such an opportunity, and triggered a round. Even with his ears plugged with cotton, the shotgun's roar was deafening as it twisted and snorted and bucked again when Iggy tugged on the trigger, then looked to see what he had wrought.

Not what he expected. The Gibbs car was nowhere to be seen.

"Leontine?" Connor Gibbs said as they had pulled up to the red light. "Do exactly what I tell you, and nothing else."

Leontine's heart was in her throat, but she nodded her acquiescence.

"Coming up behind us, on the left, is a Dodge sedan. I think the driver's one of those gents I communed with outside your home."

"What are you going to do?"

"When I hit the gas, you go between the seats like lightning and cover Jared with your body."

"But—"

"No buts. Do it."

"Yes. Okay. I will. Oh my God."

They sat docilely as if waiting for the light to change, then as the Dodge pulled up beside them, Gibbs suddenly stomped the gas pedal and off they went.

Backward.

"WHAT THE FUCK!" Iggy Cremins exclaimed in extreme befuddlement at Gibbs's sudden disappearance, and fired off a third shot. Alas, the recoil from the preceding two had caused the shotgun to slip in his grasp, and the muzzle to point more skyward than Iggy might have wished. The result was that his third dose removed part of the car's headliner, a goodly chunk from the passenger-side door frame, and an arthritic wristbone from an elderly man sitting in the park beside the Fabric Menagerie. The old man yelped, and his upper plate fell to the ground as Iggy regained a modicum of composure, found reverse, and hustled after Gibbs. It was a good thing traffic was light.

Jared was voicing his objection to the din, the rough ride, and his mother's suffocating *presence*. "WAHHH!" he proclaimed, or something to that effect. "Right on, little man!" Gibbs concurred from the front seat, burning rubber as he backed swiftly past the Cinema on Main and careened onto Franklin, heading west, with the Intrepid in hot pursuit. A diner was just leaving Young's Pizza Parlor as Gibbs and Iggy roared past. Fortunately, she was quick on her feet.

"Uh-oh," Gibbs groaned from the front seat.

"What do you mean, uh-oh!" Leontine yelled from the backseat.

"WAHHH!" Jared expleted from the car seat.

And the Sienna reined itself in, screeched onto North South Street, nearly on two wheels, then, just as its suspension had taken a set, cut a slashing right onto West Pine, at the Neighbors Citgo, and roared east.

On came the Dodge.

South on 52 went the cars, weaving frantically in and out, irate drivers honking and gesturing obscenely, forcing an ancient Escort onto the verge near Big Lots, until Connor hung an exit at Holly Springs Church Road, then a curve and a ninety-degree right onto old U.S. 52, then a sharp left-hander onto Sheep Farm Road with Iggy right up his tailpipe. Not good. Then *Ha*! and the Dodge overcooked the turn and slid sideways into a yard, giving Connor breathing room. Taking advantage of it, Gibbs floored the pedal.

A curve to starboard next, then one to port, a mobile home not far off the road at its apex, then a curve again, with the winding blacktop now separating a field on one side from a narrow finger of woods on the other. Abruptly, Gibbs did a moonshiner's turn—180 degrees, ending in the exact center of the road facing the way they had just come—and hit the glove compartment release. Inside, a Colt .45 auto. Connor retrieved it and quit the car, racking a shell into its chamber, as he did so hollering to Leontine: "Get out!"

Leontine had already loosed her braying child and had one foot out the door, but when Gibbs yelled at her she turned up the wick. In five seconds, she was yards away from the car, scampering into the thin but sheltering copse.

Gibbs, pistol at his side, stood twenty feet in front of his Toyota and waited for the intrepid Intrepid.

Iggy Cremins had barely managed to keep his nose to the Gibbs back bumper—despite his Dodge's considerable advantage over the Sienna in power and handling—until that freaking curve back there had nearly wiped him out. *So where's Gibbs now*? he thought, his tires shoveling sparse winter turf as he careened onto the road.

"There!" he shouted in exhilaration. Off he roared in pursuit.

As he took a second curve too fast—but holding the road this time—he was suddenly aggrieved to see Gibbs standing in front of the Toyota, athwart the centerline, bringing a handgun to bear.

It was the last thing Iggy ever saw clearly. His Dodge left the road at seventy-five miles an hour and impacted a large pine tree at sixty. No one knows how fast Iggy himself was going when a stout pine branch shattered the windshield, skewered his face, and scrambled his aberrant brain.

Chapter 27

"AND HOW COULD YOU BE CERTAIN THIS MAN wanted to kill you?"

"He shot at me. Well, at us."

"With what?"

"A gun," Gibbs replied.

The North Carolina Highway Patrol officer gave Connor Gibbs a stern look, not his first during the brief interview, but rather than being intimidated, Gibbs appeared bored. Leontine Chevalier had finally calmed a distraught Jared and was seated in the Toyota Sienna, now parked safely by the side of the road.

"Can you be more specific?"

"Shotgun. Twelve gauge. Short barrel. Semi-auto."

"How do you know it was an autoloader?"

"He used only one hand. Hard to do that with a pump, especially in a vehicle. Not impossible though. Once, in Honduras—"

"So," the officer interrupted, "you engaged in this wild chase."

"Not a chase, an elusion. I was the chasee. Along with the lady there, and Jared."

"So you deliberately endangered the lives of two people."

"I confess."

"What?"

"I confess, write me up. Or arrest me. But stop talking at me. That's cruel and unusual punishment. Besides, I haven't been convicted, yet. Or even tried. My guess is I won't be, either tried or convicted. But you go ahead and ticket me anyway, it'll look great on your record. Let's see, there's going the wrong way down a one-way street, making an unsafe move, speeding, reckless endangerment, running a stop sign, failure to yield, careless and reckless, insulting an officer—"

"When did you insult an officer?"

"Soon. Very soon."

And then the Sheriff's Department entered Sheep Farm Road, sirens wailing.

"Don't give a purple turd who had the greatest all-time batting average, I got my money on Green Bay this week. It's near 'bout Christmas, ain't you heard? Baseball's over." It was Deputy Number One, speaking into his microphone.

"Baseball's never over," quipped Deputy Number Two, in a second car, also into his handset. "Just dormant."

"Like a groun'hog?"

"Ten bucks says you can't come up with the right name."

"I s'pose it was Mickey Klutz," Number One elided.

"Oakland A's, 1978," from Number Two.

"Batted a thousand, ol' Mick," Number One agreed as his lights flashed and his siren screamed.

"Right, and batted only *twice*. Who's tops with, say, at least 400 at-bats?"

More wailing and flashing as Number One pondered. "Rogers Hornsby, St. Louis, 19-and-24," he offered.

Nothing but static over the radio.

"Well?" demanded Deputy Number One, sliding to a halt beside a Highway Patrol car.

"Wrong," asserted Number Two, also screeching to a stop. "Hornsby hit .424. Not good enough."

"Then who, dammit?" said Number One, and hitched his gunbelt.

"Ask Beaufort," Number Two laughed, and got out of his car.

"What you doin', Harris?" said Deputy Number One.

"Waiting for you boys. Need help on this one," answered Highway Patrolman Harris Beaufort. "It's a biggie."

"Well, we're here now. You can go," from Deputy Two.

"It's a fatality, gentlemen, and this man's involved." Beaufort tossed a thumb at Connor Gibbs, currently leaning against Beaufort's patrolman's car, heavy arms and legs crossed, eyes half-lidded.

"You softened him up, for sure. Is he petrified from fear, or about to fall asleep?"

Beaufort straightened his tie. "I've got him on at least a dozen charges, beginning with—"

"You see him c'mit any? With your own eyes?" asked Deputy Number One.

Beaufort shook his head. "No, but he admitted—"

"On tape?" said Number Two.

"No, but—"

"See you, Beaufort," from Deputy Number Two, and he strolled over toward Gibbs.

Deputy One, stopping momentarily as he passed Harris Beaufort, said low-voiced, "Worth a fin to me to know who has the highest all-time baseball batting average."

"Up yours," said the Highway Patrolman, turning on his heel.

"Always heard that about you State boys," Number One cracked and joined his partner.

Chapter 28

"ALL THAT JUST TO KEEP FROM PAYING ME TEN bucks," Rae said from the other end of the connection.

"Hey," Gibbs objected, sitting in his car now, after having discussed the situation with the deputies. "I burned fifty bucks off my tires during the chase. By the way, I'm not far from your house. Will you give me the once-over there?"

"When?"

"Whenever the authorities let me leave."

"Give me a clue, I got ribs on."

"With garlic, and some of that special sauce? Do you still—?"

"Connor?"

"What?"

"For you even to discuss food after seeing a man die is icky."

"Icky?"

"Icky."

"But he tried to *shoot me*. And a woman. And her baby."

"Baby?" said a suddenly worried Rae.

"Yes."

"What are you into this time, Connor Gibbs?"

"While you cut my hair, I'll tell you all about it."

So later Rae clipped, and Connor talked, and Leontine Chevalier sat in Rae's kitchen and watched and listened, and marveled at the man Connor Gibbs.

And how nicely he fit into her plans.

Chapter 29

EDDIE CHEVALIER WAS CERTAIN OF TWO THINGS: he hated New Jersey, and he missed his mama. Despite the best efforts of his Aunt LouAnne and her children to make him feel at home, Eddie was miserable. Although Aunt LouAnne jokingly told him that Santa Claus would find him in Westampton, he knew that her earnings were already spread thin enough, that the last thing she needed was another kid to provide for, and that there was no Santa anyway. But he went along with her, smiling and cutting up just as if he weren't dying inside.

LouAnne was currently snoring on the couch, dead beat after a long day, with the TV set softly blaring and the greasy smells of supper lingering in the air. Eddie lay on his back in the big master bed, which he shared with cousin Sack, tall and wide and currently muttering in his sleep. Eddie was envious of anyone who could sleep like that, and he was tempted to toss a disturbing elbow to stir his cousin, but decided against it. That would be petty, and Eddie wasn't petty. Lonely, yes. But not petty.

So he stared at the dark ceiling until eventually sleep came, after a fashion.

• • •

"You wrote your father once this week already," barked Felicia Gibbs.

Cameron looked up from his desk. "I like to write him. You won't let me call him. Besides, I finished all my homework."

Felicia swung her head, lips curled disdainfully. "Look at this room. Looks like a family of migrant workers lives in here. Clean it up."

"In a minute, okay?"

Felicia jerked the letter from under Cameron's hand. "Now!" She tore the missive in half, tossed it in the trash, and whirled from the room, hating her sorry ex-husband and harboring strong resentment against her son.

He was far too much like his dad.

Cody Wainright McGraw, otherwise known as Blister, lay on his bed stroking Zepper—the Boykin spaniel Connor Gibbs had given him—and ruminating. Zepper lay hard against the boy's hip as the radio played softly. Vera was moving somewhere within the house.

Connor's going to need help with this case, there are just too many against him. Bennie can't be around all the time, or Mr. Crenshaw, and that Chiles man gives me the creeps, though I'm not sure why, he always acts polite, and smiles easily, but there's something . . . off *about him.*

Well, Connor had once helped Blister find his daddy, and earned a stay in the hospital for his trouble. Now Cody McGraw might be in a position to repay that debt.

But how?

He stroked Zepper's brown coat until he fell asleep.

Johnny Applewhite lay on his side. Because his back hurt. Drunk as a miner, Uncle Anson had overdone the whipping tonight, leaving the boy not only cowed and hurting, but bleeding.

But not crying.

Never again would Anson make him cry, vowed the boy, as he lay prostrate, biting his pillow against the pain.

Chapter 30

"WHERE?" SAID GANTT HELMS, A GLOB OF tapioca on his upper lip.

"Mount Airy," said brother Sherman.

"What hospital?" Gantt's broad tongue searched the spoon for residue.

"Hell, Gantt, there probably isn't more than one in a town that size."

"WELL, SEND SOMEONE!"

So Sherman made a call."

"Where?" said Estelle Lawson.

"Mount Airy," Gibbs replied.

"I've never even been to Mount Airy, let alone know any cops there. Hey, isn't that where Andy Griffith—?"

"Yes. Well, if you don't have any pull with the local sheriff, could you call Holmes for me?"

"Where are you?"

"At a friend's, lady who cuts my hair. There's a deputy planted outside to make sure I don't sneak off."

"And all this happened this morning?"

"Right. Leontine and I have been at Rae's for a couple of

hours, but I need freedom of movement. My watchdog hampers it."

"You think?" Estelle said, then, "I'll get back to you."

An hour later, she did. No dice. Apparently the Surry County Sheriff's Department was squeaky clean and tough to influence.

"I'll be in touch," said Connor Gibbs. "Thanks for trying."

"Connor?"

"See you later, bye."

"Connor!"

But he was gone.

"I'll call Bennie," Connor told Rae and Leontine. "I have a plan."

"Am I involved?" Rae asked.

"Would I involve you?" said Connor.

"I have to live in this town, Connor," Rae protested.

Connor nodded in commiseration.

Rae sighed. "What do I have to do?"

Connor told her.

"You have the baby with you?" Benella said.

"Who was I going to leave him with?" Connor protested.

"Me."

"You had an aerobics class."

"We also have a nursery at the gym, and you know it."

"You going to come or not?"

"What do you think?"

So he explained the plan. Benella listened attentively and seventy-three minutes later was exactly where Connor had instructed her to be.

"I may be able to dump a little political pressure on the Surry County Sheriff's Department, if you think it'd help," offered Holmes Crenshaw. "Client of mine was a big contributor in the last election."

"I hear the sheriff has lots of friends in this state. Better stay clear of this unless I really need you."

"Bennie's on the way. What are you going to do in the meantime?"

"Watch an old Abbott and Costello Christmas special and eat some of Rae's pea salad," Connor said.

"Tell her I said hey."

Connor did.

Deputy Number One, whose name was Waldo Isaacs, was red-haired, portly, bored, and hungry as he watched the house from his squad car, motor running against the December chill, when Rae came out, crossed the road, motioned for him to roll down his window.

"Afternoon, Waldo," she greeted with a big smile, and nobody had a smile like Rae.

"Rae," nodded the deputy.

"You hungry?" Rae asked.

"I'm on duty is what I am."

"Your stomach still work when you're on duty?"

Isaacs feigned ambivalence, then said, "I s'pose it does, at that. What you offering?"

"Pea salad, deviled eggs, bottle of Sprite."

"Got'ny Diet Coke?"

"Sprite, Waldo."

"I reckon so, then, if that's all you got."

Rae returned to her house, then quickly brought the promised items. "Enjoy," she said, handing the provender through the squad car's open window.

As she turned away, Isaacs said, "Thanks. By the way, got'ny idea who had the highest batting average in professional baseball?"

"Sure."

"You do?" Waldo licked his lips in venal anticipation.

"You bet."

"Who?"

"I was warned you might ask me that, and told it'd be worth a fiver not to tell you."

"But, Rae . . ." whined the deputy.

"Enjoy your food," Rae said, smiled again, and hurried back across the road. She was mountain bred, but she hated the cold. And it was very cold, and the wind was up, and, as Rae reentered her front door, Connor Gibbs, Leontine Chevalier, and baby Jared were entering a thick stand of woods behind her house.

Chapter 31

THE BRIARS ARE THE WORST, LEONTINE THOUGHT. *No, this damnable mountain laurel. No, the wind, it blows right through you.* She trudged along, head down, her scanty winter coat clutched tightly to her bosom, as Connor Gibbs, a sleepy Jared cradled in his big arms, led the way. Uphill, down, slipping and sliding, rotting logs crumbling underfoot, crossing a field, another, more thicket, the laurel nearly impenetrable, then the river and its icy numbing, and more trudging, wet now, soaked to above the knee, miserable, and little conversation from the big man to pass the time.

Shit, Leontine thought, then said, her reedy voice not strong. "Helms . . . is beginning to . . . piss me off," she panted.

"Me too." He wasn't even breathing hard, the lug. How could a man that big move so easily and tirelessly? And he seemed impervious to the cold, which just made her madder.

"He could have . . . killed my baby."

"Indeed he could."

"What are you . . . planning to do . . . about it?" she wheezed, stumbling over a rock, but not falling. She angrily kicked the rock hard, not an especially intelligent thing to do, and of course hurt her toe, which did not improve her mood.

"I'm considering." Up a steep incline now, his gait never wavering. Or slowing.

"I'm tired," she groused.

"Not much farther, according to Rae."

"I need to REST!" shouted Leontine and dropped to her tuchis in the leaves.

Gibbs paused a moment. "Leontine?"

"WHAT!"

"The longer Bennie waits, the more likely she is to attract attention."

"So?" she snapped, her breathing erratic.

"I don't want attention. I want to get out of Surry County before the Sheriff decides what to do with me, if anything."

"I told you, I'm—"

Connor reached out a hand slightly smaller than a first baseman's glove, gripped Leontine by the collar of her coat, and lifted her as if she weighed only a hundred pounds, which she didn't, quite.

"Five minutes," he said. "Then you can rest all the way back to Wendover."

She batted his arm, which was akin to smacking a telephone pole with a fly swatter. But she stayed on her feet as he helped her up the incline. And five minutes later, as promised, they stepped onto a hardtop road, and there, thirty yards away, backed up to a No Trespassing sign, was parked Benella Mae Sweet, in a green BMW. She waved at them.

Rae was at the sink, washing dishes and listening to Mitch Miller and the Gang doing "Must Be Santa" on cassette, when there came a rap on her front door. Suspecting who it might be, Rae took her time drying her hands and walking to the door.

"I put the dishes there on your bench," informed Waldo

Isaacs in his nasal way, standing bareheaded there on the porch.

"Why don't you put them right here in my hands, Waldo? Then I won't have to come out and get them."

"Sorry," and Isaacs grabbed up the items, all of which were empty. Except the Sprite bottle.

"You can keep the drink," she said.

"Hate Sprite. Just used it to wash stuff down with. Tell Gibbs the sheriff called, said he can go soon's he pleases."

"Already has," from Rae, starting to close the door.

"Already has what?" Waldo asked suspiciously.

"Gone."

"Watcha mean, gone?"

"As in 'left.' You know, 'departed,' or you can choose your own word."

"Now, Rae . . ."

"Don't start with me, Waldo. I don't work for the sheriff, and my house isn't a jail. My guests come and go as they please. My customers too. Connor Gibbs is both."

"Well, shoot!" griped Waldo, hitching his belt. "The sheriff ain't gon' like this."

As he stepped off the porch, Rae said, "Waldo?"

"Yeah?" he answered, a worried frown creasing his ignoble brow.

"Hugh Duffy."

"Huh?"

"Outfielder for Boston. Hit a .438 back in 1894. No one's beaten it yet. Likely never will."

The brow uncreased itself. "No shit, I mean . . ." Waldo stumbled (Rae was a churchgoer), "gol-lee. Thanks," and back to his car he hustled, happy as a clam.

Rae closed the door and went back to her dishes.

That night, comfortable in his own house, Connor Gibbs conferred with Holmes Crenshaw, over eggnog. "They had nothing to charge you with," said Holmes. "All citizens have the right to avoid someone who's shooting at them. And there must have been fifty people who witnessed the chase at one point or another, and are willing to testify. So there'll be no charges, and no problem." He sipped his nog.

"Well, no problem from the law anyway. For now. But Gantt's something else. I'm going to have to neutralize him, and soon. He's nuts," Gibbs opined.

"I warned you about that."

Connor, settled in a big leather wingchair in the study—with its walnut paneling and Nero Wolfe–sized globe, and one wallful of books, hardcovers mostly, ranging from Richard Adams through Michael Malone to Leon Uris, and the word processor in the corner—said: "Yeah, well help me devise a way to muzzle him."

"Good choice of verbs, but I doubt you can neutralize the man. You may just have to remove him."

"This isn't Company business, Holmie. I can't simply *remove* people."

After another sip from his cup, liberally laced with usquebaugh from a pocket flask, Crenshaw mumbled, "Anymore," and at that point Benella joined them. She sat on the leather ottoman so Connor could massage her traps, and the three talked long into the night.

Chapter 32

Sherman Helms was loading a treadmill into the bed of an El Camino. Manning was helping, and sweating, despite the December cold. In the bed already were a stout logging chain and a small metal box of gunpowder capsules, the latter used to irritate a dog's stomach and make it mean. "What happened in Mount Airy?" asked Manning.

"That stupid Iggy. I told Gantt he wasn't the man for the job, but does he listen?" The chill wind whipped Sherm's hair into a nestlike shape. He turned up his collar. "Tried to take Gibbs and the bimbo out, from inside his car, on Main Street yet, and with a scattergun. Shot some geezer sitting in a park."

"And?" Manning stuck both hands in his suitcoat pocket and hunched his shoulders.

"Then there's this big chase all over the countryside, and Iggy ends up with a tree where his face used to be."

"Any way to trace it back to us?" said a worried Manning, his face beginning to turn blue.

Sherman snorted. "Who's 'us', *kemo sabe*? But no, we're not idiots. And only an idiot would have a visible connection to a jerk like Cremins." Other than having turned up his collar, Sherman showed no sign of resenting the cold.

Skinny little abnormal prick, thought Manning, but what he said was; "So what's next?"

"Gantt's got Junior and Piebald Sam on it."

It was Manning's turn to snort. "Those the two that ran over the dumpster, then later got their asses kicked by a woman?" He wiggled his fingers to keep them warm, which didn't work. They stayed stiff as frozen sausages.

"Other than our mountain friends, they're our bench."

"How's about you get Little Boy to come down from Valhalla?"

"Little Boy's too valuable. This thing with the bimbo is personal, not business. Gantt's getting a bit carried away on this, I'll admit, but not that carried away" was Sherman's assessment.

Manning remained unconvinced. "I think he needs to get this over with, or abandon it for not being worth the trouble."

"Everyone's got a right to an opinion. Only problem is nobody give's a rat's ass about yours. Stick to your own bailiwick, and your money will keep rolling in."

"Sure, Sherm, so long as the bimbo situation doesn't get out of hand."

Sherman Helms narrowed his eyes. "And if it does?"

"Then count me out," Manning said and walked stiffly away.

Junior Hughes, Junior, said, "They been in there a long time. Don't nobody never go home, sleep in their own bed?"

"Hell," opined Piebald Sam Thrippin, "maybe that spade lawyer's pairing off with the skinny broad. They could be watchin' X-rated videos and gettin' it on."

"Or maybe Gibbs is the one poking that fat-free bitch. He was staying at her trailer, y'know."

"Naw, that'd leave the lawyer with that other broad, and he ain't big enough for her."

Junior grinned. "Maybe someone could put him up to it. Get it?"

Sam didn't, but laughed anyway; what else was there to do? And they maundered thus until eventually they fell asleep.

Which was a mistake.

"Does a beige Ford Escort live three doors down?" Holmes Crenshaw, standing by Connor's living room window, asked. "Opposite side of the street?"

Connor said, "No."

"There's one parked in the drive, facing out. Two heads in it, both up front. They aren't necking."

Connor came over to look. "The Willards have never owned a Ford, especially one that small."

Crenshaw grinned, baring his canines. "Want to go for a little sashay?"

Connor sighed. "Take Bennie. I'm tired."

Benella got up from the ottoman, slipped into her coat, and said, "Could be a decoy. You know, get the starting team out of the house, then storm the place. There'd only be you to stop them."

Leontine was still asleep in the next room.

"I'll yell for help," Connor said.

So Holmes and Bennie slipped out the back.

The first thing Junior Hughes, Junior, saw upon waking was a woman standing in front of his Ford. She was awash from a street light, arms akimbo, stern of mien, and smaller than the Statue of Liberty. Slightly. He goggled, swallowed his gum, and reached for the ignition.

Too late.

• • •

In Connor Gibbs's office, on two kitchen chairs, sat a terri-
fied Junior Hughes, Junior, and a seemingly bored Piebald
Sam Thrippin. The chairs had been set on a large paint-
stained drop cloth. Junior was busy wondering why.

Gibbs, standing in front of the hapless duo, said, "Names
please."

"Up Yours and Bite Me," quipped Piebald Sam.

"Are you Up or Bite?" from Gibbs.

"What's the drop cloth for?" asked Junior Hughes, Junior,
looking down at the mentioned item and shuffling his feet.

Piebald Sam looked over at Junior and said, "Whaddya
think, stupid?"

Bristling, Junior said, "I told you not to call me stoopit."

"The drop cloth is to make it easier to clean up the mess,"
said Benella Mae from across the room.

"What mess?" chirped a dismayed Junior Hughes, Junior.

"The mess that is going to be on the floor if you fellows
don't impress us with your knowledge," Connor threatened.

At that point Holmes Crenshaw came into the room carrying a table lamp. Its shade and bulb had been removed; its
cord was being dragged across the hardwood floor. Crenshaw said, "This the lamp you wanted?" to Gibbs.

"No, but it'll do," Gibbs allowed.

"For what!" shouted Junior.

"Shut *up*!" hissed Piebald Sam.

"Just plug it in behind the desk there," Connor instructed.

Holmes did, then handed Gibbs the lamp. "What if it kills
him?" Holmes muttered, just loud enough.

"Didn't kill that guy in Kosovo."

"European current's different," from Crenshaw.

"Let's see," said Gibbs. "Who first?"

"The tough one," Benella said, pointing at Piebald Sam.
"I want to hear him yell."

"Wait a minute—" Junior began.

But Piebald Sam cut him off with "Shut the fuck *UP*!"

"He's the wuss," Crenshaw proclaimed, speaking of Junior Hughes, Junior. "Do him first."

"Whaddya want to know?" screeched Junior, overcome by fear, just as Piebald Sam lunged from his chair. Connor decked him with a hard right to the chin. Piebald Sam stayed on the floor, unconscious.

Connor turned his attention to Junior. "Guess that means you go first."

Junior couldn't summon sufficient spit to swallow.

"Help me get his pants off," Holmes said, motioning to Junior. Then, "Bennie, bring some cotton balls from the bathroom. We'll stuff them in his mouth so the neighbors won't hear him scream."

Benella was only halfway across the room when Junior Hughes, Junior, began to talk.

And talk.

Connor was on the phone with Braxton Chiles, saying, "Do you know of a fellow named Little Boy?"

"You bet I do, my man," Braxton affirmed. "He's the head of Gantt's western division, and a very competent dude."

"Hombre by the name of Up Yours told me that Gantt might bring Mr. Boy in on this thing with Leontine."

"That is bad news, my friend."

"Tough is he, this Little Boy?"

"Tough doesn't adequately describe him. He's from near Black Mountain, I understand, real name Robert Benton Kew, part Indian or something. Folks called him Bobby as a boy. Then the mean kids began to call him Bobby Kew, big joke, until he was eight or so and hit a growth spurt. No more Bobby Kew. You know that ole redneck song from the sixties? '. . . and a crashin' blow from a huge right hand,' sent some guy to the Promised Land, I dunno the lyrics? Well, with Little Boy it was two guys, one punch apiece. Of

course he knows where to hit. Former Green Beret or something."

"I assume he's called Little Boy because of his size?"

"He's one big mother, Connor, even bigger than you.
Not taller, in fact maybe an inch or two shy, but he's wide
as the Dean Dome and near as weighty. And quick. Worked
his way through college playing racquetball with the mon-
eyed crowd, betting on himself. Can you imagine a 280-
odd-pound racquetball whiz? I can't. And strong. In the
all-South powerlifting meet five years ago, he deadlifted
right at four hundred kilos. You know how much that is in
pounds."

Connor whistled softly in admiration.

"Right. Don't joust with this mug. He would hurt you."

"Where is he now?"

"Outside Jefferson, overseeing Gantt's vast weed produc-
tion, not to mention his car theft ring and pooch-fighting
empire. By the way, there's another Gantt subordinate up
mountainward, gent hangs his hat on the sobriquet Pepperoy
Jenesais-Quoi. He's a dog trainer out of Canada by way of
Jolliet Prison in Illinois. A blade man, but even-tempered.
Like a wolverine is even-tempered, always mad. Quiet
though, and a good singing voice. I hear he sounds like
Eddie Fisher with a Canuck accent."

"How about someone by the name of Slide Websen?"

"Gantt's go between. Spends half his life on Highway
421, back and forth. He's a money man, and a gofer, but no
heavy lifting. Fancies himself, and thirteen-year-old boys.
Has a kiddie-porn venture on the side, out of a loft in Charlotte. Gantt doesn't know."

"Does Little Boy?"

"Hell no. He'd crush Slide's larynx. Or some other body
part."

"Maybe Little Boy isn't so bad."

"Not mean bad, just *bad* bad, if you know what I mean.

Like you, he's honorable. It's just that petty legalities don't trouble him much," Chiles finished.

"Thanks, Braxton."

"Do I start getting a stipend?"

"Sure. We'll call it a wedding gift."

Braxton Chiles blushed as he hung up the phone.

Chapter 33

"So WHAT'S NEXT, SUGAR PIE?" THE HOUSE WAS quiet. Leontine and Jared were sound asnooze, and Holmes Crenshaw had gone home. Connor and Benella lay naked on the bed, each covered with the thin sheen of exertion.

"Set Gantt up for removal," Gibbs replied.

Benella adjusted her position—shift of leg here, an arm there, tilt of head, the fall of amber tresses upon ample curves. She ended by placing one of his hands on a breast.

"How?" she asked finally.

"I'm working on that."

"Am I involved?"

"Not if I can help it."

"Will it be rough sledding?"

"Probably."

"Then you can't keep me out of it. I will safeguard my sweet patootie at all costs."

"You've proven that in the past."

She nuzzled his thick shoulder. "As have you."

"We make a good team."

"We make good whoopee, too." She nibbled his nape and giggled.

Looking deep into her effulgent face, he said, "And how."
So they did. Again.

Hours later, with Connor and Benella sleeping upstairs, Leontine went on a fridge raid. Over strawberry ice cream, she sat deep in thought.

She might have to do it herself after all. That Amazon had a hold on Gibbs, literally and metaphorically, and Leontine doubted she could compete.

Oh well. She'd just have to change plans.

Hundreds of miles north, at 3:32 in the morning, Eddie Chevalier came to a decision. It required implementation.

So he implemented it.

At 4:17 that same morning, Junior Hughes, Junior, and his cousin Piebald Sam Thrippin pointed their Escort south and west, filled to the gills and bound for kith and kin in Alabama. Sam's jaw hurt, but not as badly as his whole body would if Gantt Helms found out the full extent of Junior's recitation. The very thought made Sam shiver, so he nudged the little Ford up to 80 and set the cruise.

Chapter 34

GANTT HELMS WAS DOING HIS SLOW BURN ROU-
tine. Which was good. Gantt wasn't as dangerously precipi-
tous as when fully enraged. Still, brother Sherm knew the
ice was thin.

"Gone?" said Gantt, raising an eyebrow. He sat poolside.
A lukewarm beer sat Ganttside. Rolls of fat spilled over,
white and fishlike and repugnant. Tom Cruise he was not.

"Gone. Vanished. As in disappeared," said Sherman.
"Took all their stuff with them."

"Stuff?"

"You know . . . underwear, VCR, guns, ammo, coat hang-
ers, CDs, soap, hair spray—"

Up went Gantt's other brow. "They took our coat hang-
ers?"

"Just kidding, bro. What I mean is that they didn't take
off on a weekend skiing trip. They scattered to the wind."
He was speaking of Piebald Sam and Junior Hughes, Junior.

Gantt took a sip of lukewarm beer and licked his lips. He
looked over at the Jewel, lying on a thick comforter not far

away, her leonine head up and alert, watching over Master. "Well now," he said.

Sherm waited, but naught was forthcoming. After nearly a minute, he said, "What do you mean, 'well now'?"

But Gantt was lost in thought.

So Sherman left, cloaked in foreboding.

As soon as the door clicked behind the departing brother Sherm, Gantt pressed a button.

"Yeah?" It was Detective Manning, from the kitchen, sounding tinny over the intercom.

"I want to talk with Braxton Chiles," Gantt said.

"Where?"

"Here, asshole."

Manning, five rooms away, took a big breath, held it, let it out slowly through his nose. Then, "Chiles won't come here."

"Then go get him." Another gulp of beer as the Jewel watched.

"Not for what you pay me."

"Aw, for Pete's . . . all right, set up a meet someplace."

"Where?"

"I don't give a . . . no wait . . . make it a restaurant, one that requires a tie. That'll needle him."

"Needling Braxton Chiles is a bad idea."

"Fuck him, and fuck *you!*" Gantt's slow burn was evaporating. "Do what I said!" he shouted and switched off the intercom.

"Chiles Enterprises. How may I help you?" came the voice.

Manning said, "Put Chiles on the phone."

"And whom may I say is calling?"

Manning said, "The guy who's gonna deviate your septum if you don't put him on the fucking phone."

CLICK.

Manning said, "Sonuvabitch!" into the dead phone, then drew in a huge draft to oxygenate his system, letting it slowly seep out through his neb. Then he hit Redial.

"Chiles Enterprises. How may I help you?" The same cheerful voice.

Manning said, "I'd like to speak with Braxton Chiles."

"And whom may I say is calling?"

"Detective Manning."

"Danny Manning?"

"*Detective* Danny Manning."

"Say 'please.' "

"What!"

"Say '*please*.' "

"Look, you little weasel—"

CLICK.

Manning withdrew from a cabinet a bottle of Dewar's, and made a serious dent in it before calling again.

When Thorton Chiles hung up the phone, chuckling for the second time, Braxton looked up from his chess board and queried, "What's so amusing?" The pair was seated in a warehouse owned by Braxton, in a rundown part of town. The room was furnished with two desks, two metal file cabinets, two chairs, a *Sports Illustrated* swimsuit cover (laminated and thumb-tacked to the wall), two floor lamps, and a calico named Ruby, currently asleep. Dust mites played.

"That freaking Danny Manning," Thorton answered, still grinning.

"Don't cuss. You're not old enough."

" 'Freaking' isn't cussing," the teen objected.

"It's close enough. So what did he want?" asked Braxton Chiles.

"To speak to you."

Braxton moved a white rook to Q6. "Wonder what Br'er Manning wants with little old me," he mused aloud.

"A challenge match? Maybe he just rented *Searching for Bobby Fischer.*"

Braxton simply grunted and moved a black pawn. When the phone rang again, some time later, he answered it himself. Thorton was in the bathroom.

Chapter 35

THE RESTAURANT SPECIALIZED IN CHINESE CUIsine and was expansive and crowded. The diminutive maitre d' looked Braxton Chiles over suspiciously, not so much due to the aqua leisure suit but to the fact that Braxton's polka-dotted tie had two holes in it. Surrounded by black smudges. They appeared to be bullet holes.

"Nice tie," observed the maitre d', the top of his shaved head somewhere in the vicinity of Braxton's chin.

"Bought it off a quick-draw artist, fan of *Gunsmoke* reruns. Shot himself accidentally," Chiles said remorsefully.

"Twice?"

"He was a bad shot."

The maitre d' smiled thinly and spun on his size-seven heels, motioning Braxton Chiles to follow. At the rear of the room, Gantt Helms was at a table, surrounded by dishes piled high with steaming provender, his ample mouth at that very moment taking in a fresh supply. At his elbow stood Detective Danny Manning, the obvious bulge of a gun on his hip. At Gantt's feet lay the Jewel. Draped over her thick body was a knitted orange sweater proclaiming that she was an ASSISTANCE DOG. At Chiles's approach, Manning stepped forward, his hands beginning to reach for Braxton's jacket.

"Nope," said Braxton Chiles, stopping Manning's hands mid-reach.

"I gotta frisk you."

"No you don't. I have a gun. Two in fact."

"Then you can't—"

"He called me, remember?" from Chiles, as the Jewel's head came around and met his eyes. There on the floor was the menace, not this self-important civil servant.

Still ten feet away from Jewel, Chiles spoke softly to Gantt Helms. "Move the dog."

Gantt was busy chewing, but he heard Chiles and lifted a hand. The Jewel elevated easily and moved, clearing the way for Braxton to seat himself at the table. She lay down again, a dozen feet away.

Braxton said, "I've got a SIG .45 in my hand, under the table so it won't spoil your appetite. If that dog so much as scratches a flea, I'll put two Hydra-Shok hollow points up your pee-pee. The rest of them will go into the mutt. Probably all of us will die, but you first, and hard. You dig?"

Gantt nodded, his fat cheeks filled with food, and pushed a thick envelope across the tabletop. Chiles took it left-handed, opened it the same way. Inside were many hundred-dollar bills. "How much?" Chiles asked.

"Ten grand," answered Helms, the words muffled by partially masticated food.

"Just for having dinner with you?"

Helms snorted through the mouthful, chewed it down to swallowing size, then said, "Down payment on fifty, total." He took a swig of hot tea from a thimble-sized cup.

"For killing whom?"

Helms laughed. "Does it matter?"

"Sure. For example, my mom is off limits."

Gantt Helms skewered Chiles with a porcine look. "Connor Gibbs."

"Oh, him. Sure. No problem."

Up came the bushy brows, both at once, indicating genuine surprise. "*Gibbs* ain't no problem?"

"The bigger they are, the easier to hit."

Gantt shrugged. "The ten's to consummate the deal. Other forty when it's done," said Helms before taking on a forkful of rice.

"Sure. Is there a schedule?"

"Sooner."

"Okay."

"So the deal's done?" from Gantt.

Braxton nodded his lean head.

"Don't try to fuck me, Chiles. I'd take it bad."

"So would I, my man. So would I."

Chapter 36

CHRISTMAS IN LOS ANGELES WASN'T VERY MUCH like Christmas, at least not to Cameron Gibbs. And he missed his father. A lot. But his mother had full custody and wouldn't even let Cameron visit his dad, let alone live with him. And Connor couldn't come get him; then he'd be in trouble with the law. Maybe even for kidnapping, who knows.

So what to do?

What if he slipped one of his mother's credit cards out of her purse, and used it to buy a plane ticket? No, not a good idea; airports had too much security. A bus, then. Or train.

Better.

And so he plotted.

"Fourteen dollars even, for the gas," said Anson Applewhite. "Seventy-five cents for the Nabs."

Little Boy handed him a twenty, and Applewhite gave change.

"Where's Johnny?" asked Little Boy. "Haven't seen him in a couple days."

"Dunno," Anson lied. "Prob'ly up to no good with some of his worthless pals."

No, he wasn't, and Anson knew it. The boy was locked in the basement. And he was listening. But Anson didn't know that.

"Where you headed?" Applewhite asked Little Boy.

The big man just turned away; it was none of the store-keep's business where he was headed. "I'll be gone a few days. Tell Johnny I said bye."

"Sure," Anson replied, waving a hand, though he had no intention of telling Johnny anything.

Johnny meanwhile, having heard that Little Boy was leaving town, scrambled to where there was a loose board in the wall. Within five minutes he'd pried it loose, then another, and was wriggling through the opening into daylight. Little Boy hadn't left yet; his truck was parked outside the hangar-sized garage. So Johnny jumped into its bed and under a tarp, to hunker there, shivering. It would be a long drive, and cold. But worth it. He'd tell Little Boy about the most recent beating and that he'd never go back to his uncle, and then Little Boy would find a place for him to live, some-where, with folks who didn't hit . . .

Maybe with Little Boy himself.

At least he didn't hit kids.

Holmes Crenshaw said, "Here's your gun," and handed Leontine her Charter Arms revolver. She was seated on the living room sofa, stringing colored beads for decoration, but took the gun and slipped it beneath a cushion.

"That way," Holmes continued, "you can fill Gantt Helms full of holes if he comes after you."

Leontine smiled and nodded her appreciation, all the while thinking, *Or if I go after him.*

Connor was in the basement, bench pressing. Free weights. Four-hundred pounds. Four reps. He said, "Hey, Holmie," as Crenshaw came down the stairs.

"Hi. Need a spot?"

"No, but I will let you do them for me," groaned a red-faced Gibbs, then racked the bar with a heavy *clang*! He sat up and rotated his arms to loosen his shoulders; benches can be tough on joints.

"Do some towel dislocates. Your joints will never ache," Holmes advised.

"Want me to cut the weight in half so you can do some?"

"Haw. I worked on the Nautilus this morning, an hour and a half."

"With how much?"

"Never mind. I'm not an animal. By the way, got Leontine's gun back from the po-leece. No ammunition, though. We'll have to buy her some."

Connor stared into space. "I'm not so sure."

"Hey, she can't live here forever. Not unless you marry her. Maybe not even then, hard as you are to live with."

"We'll see," said Connor, then lay back to do his third set of benches.

"Mr. Abernathy?"

"Yo."

"This is Connor's friend, Leontine Chevalier."

"Yo."

"I'm staying at his house now. For a while."

"Can I do for you?"

"I need some bullets."

"I assume you mean cartridges."

"I think so."

"What caliber?"

"Thirty-eight Special."

"Hollow points?"

"Will they do more damage?"

"Damn right."

"Then get me those."

"Plus-P?"

"I beg your pardon?"

"Hot loads?"

"Do they kick more?"

"You bet."

"I . . . guess so."

"Treasury load, or the heavy bullet stuff?"

"Which is better?"

"The lighter bullets don't penetrate as much, but expand more."

"Is that better?"

"Depends."

"Then you choose."

"You going after man, or beast?"

"Both," she said.

"I'll drop some by in an hour."

"Put them in the mailbox."

Silence then, a few seconds of absorption. "Forty bucks."

"I'll put two twenties in the box. But the mail runs early in the afternoon."

"I said an hour, that's what I meant. See that the money's there."

"I will," she said and hung up.

She put Connor's Rolodex back in the drawer, withdrew a pair of twenties from her purse, took them to the mailbox. Fifty minutes later she saw a Corvette approach, stop briefly at the box, then rumble away.

After fifty-three minutes total, her Charter Arms was fully loaded.

Eddie Chevalier had been eating donuts every day at the truck stop since he'd come to New Jersey. He enjoyed talking to the truckers. And they, probably missing their own kids, seemed to enjoy talking to him. One in particular, a tall Irishman who made a mail run from Trenton to Charlotte every other night. Slipping into the back of that truck would be a piece of cake, and Charlotte was less than a hundred miles from Wendover.

So when Eddie spotted the truck, he slipped in, found a small, comfortable spot to curl up, and went to sleep.

The Irishman was disappointed that he didn't get to talk to little Eddie, even hung around longer than he should on the chance that the kid might show up. Then, looking at his watch one last time, he paid his tab and shoved off.

With Eddie fast asleep in the back of his rig.

Chapter 37

GANTT WAS ON HIS INDOOR PUTTING GREEN, putting, and vaguely reminiscent of a rhinoceros in plaid shorts, only not as cute. He missed the shot and threw his putter across the room, where something broke noisily. "Well, FUCK!" he erupted.

Slide Websen examined his fingernails; the cuticles needed work.

"So, what you got for me?" Helms said.

"A sister-in-law in Westampton, New Jersey, a cousin clear out in Pocatello, and an uncle in Dallas."

"Where the hell is Pocatello?"

"Idaho."

"Hell, Slide, I don't have unlimited resources. We can't check 'em all." He clumped across the room to examine the damage done by his putter. "Hey, that's a break."

"What's a break?"

"Club hit that picture of my mother. Been looking for an excuse to toss that, one that Sherm would buy. Now I got one. Ugly old bitch."

"What do I do next?" from Websen.

"Boz Fangelli owes me for that Jag I got his wife. Call

him, tell him to put one of his Yankee relatives to work for a change. Get me a line on this cunt up in Jersey, see does she have a new kid around."

"What about the others?"

Gantt tossed him a look. "Just do what I said. New Jersey's closer, and that Chevalier bimbo ain't made of money. Lives in a fucking trailer, you know."

Websen went to do as bidden.

Estelle Lawson answered the second ring. "Detective Lawson."

"Hi, Essie."

She smiled in spite of herself. "No one's called me Essie in a month of Super Bowl Sundays."

"How've you been?"

The smile went away. "Now's a fine time to go wondering."

Ten seconds of line hum, then, "We were no good, darlin'. You were on the fast track to a gold shield, and Larry was pushing you hard, and . . ."

"And what?"

"I tend to go my own way, y'know."

She sighed. Because she did indeed know.

"How is Larry, by the way?"

"Gone. Men don't seem to be much for sticking it out."

Another long pause. "So . . . who's in your life now?"

She laughed. "Forget it, Bobby-B. I'm not into romancing long distance, especially with convicted felons."

"That was tossed out of court, darlin'. I'm rap free, except for a coupla speeding tickets."

"Taxation by citation."

"Hey, I like that."

"So, what do you want, cupcake?"

"Can't I just be checking up on an old friend?"

"After eleven years? I don't think so."

So Bobby-B told her what he wanted.

It made her blood run cold.

The wino could always be found on the corner of Fifth and Franklin, with a sign suggesting that work might be exchanged for food. Oddly, or so it had always seemed to Cameron, the wino was always moderately well dressed. For a wino. The wino said, "Any money today, boy?"

"Maybe," Cameron Gibbs said. "But you'll have to work for it."

Chuckling, the wino said, "What's in you mind, boy?"

After Cameron had explained what he wanted, the wino said, "And I get fifty bucks, plus you cover the taxi fare to and fro?"

"That's right."

"Give me twenty now, and you pay the cab both ways, right up front. The cabbie can wait for me," bargained the wino.

"Okay," Cameron agreed and handed over a twenty, one of the old ones that don't look like Monopoly money.

The wino snatched it away, stuck it in a pocket, and whistled loudly for a taxi. In minutes, they were on their redolent way.

Eddie Chevalier was doing some fast talking. His Irish friend had caught him asleep in the back of the tractor trailer, and the man was scared to death.

"But it's not your fault. I'm the one sneaked into your truck," Eddie blurted.

"Aye, but do ya think th' authorities will give a care about that?"

"Put me on a bus to my mom in Wendover, and I'll be out of your hair. I've got almost ten dollars saved up." For validation, he held out the money, most of it ones.

The trucker couldn't help but smile. "Lad, you'll not buy

a ticket to much of anywhere for that kind of jack. But come with me and we'll test the lay of the land."

An hour later, the trucker having provided the fare, Eddie Chevalier was on his way to Wendover, by Greyhound.

He had a good seat.

The wino took Cameron's credit card—more correctly, Felicia's credit card—and slid it across the counter. Cameron fidgeted until the deal was done and the wino had reacquired the plastic. Finally, with ticket and boarding pass in hand, he said, "May I have the card, please?"

The wino hesitated. "I can do a lot with this card, boy. Fix up my digs."

"Not if I call it in stolen as soon as you leave."

The wino laughed at that. "And then I'll report you little scam to the airport police."

"But you signed the receipt. And with someone else's name. That's fraud. Besides, they don't put ten-year-olds in jail, especially in California. Middle-aged street people is another story."

The wino laughed again. "Middle-aged is it?" She was at least sixty-five, and looked every year of it. "How tactful."

She held out her thin, blue-veined hand, trembling slightly, and the boy shook it. "We make a good team. My name's Jennie, what's yours?"

"Cameron."

"Well, Cameron, here's your card."

Young Gibbs pocketed the plastic and proffered the thirty dollars he owed. Jennie took it. "If you ever make it back to L.A. . . ." she said.

"Take care," from Cameron.

Then he was gone.

Chapter 38

THE SHORT, STOCKY DETECTIVE WAS OFF DUTY and on the case. The Connor Gibbs case. Since Estelle Lawson would never have sanctioned such surveillance—not on Gibbs—the dick was doing it on his own time. He'd get something on the big bruiser, one way or another, if he had to work at it six months. Besides, what else did he have to do? He had no wife, no social life, no friends, no hobbies. Except one, and that he could do on stakeout. So he did, slipping on his Walkman earphones. The sounds of Bluegrass filled his ears.

Twenty minutes later, half asleep, he sat up abruptly, thinking, *What the hell*?

It was Detective Estelle Lawson, going into Connor Gibbs's home.

Well shut my mouth, thought the squat dick, and removed the Walkman.

They settled under the big Christmas tree in the living room, Estelle in the leather wing chair, Gibbs on the sofa. Estelle sipped at her brandy, but clearly her heart wasn't in it.

"What is it, Stelle?"

After a third sip, she said, "Do you know a man named Robert Kew? He used to be called Bobby."

"Now he goes by Little Boy."

"I hadn't heard that."

"Like the bomb."

"The what?" She sipped again.

"The atomic bomb."

"Oh, right." Another sip. "Apt, I must say."

"Explosive, is he?"

"Not really. Just capable of heavy damage. Very heavy."

Gibbs nodded. "I've heard. What about Mr. Kew?"

"He called me. An hour ago." She looked at him worriedly. "He wants a meet. With you."

Gibbs nodded. "Ditto."

"No you don't. He is very upset, Connor."

Gibbs hiked a brow, Rhett Butler style. "About what?"

"Bingo."

"I'm not especially happy about that either."

Estelle drained her glass. "This is not a good idea, but if you insist on a conference, face to face, I'll chaperone."

"No."

"Connor—"

"Sorry, Stelle. Where does he want to hold this palaver?"

She told him.

Johnny Applewhite was freezing. Literally. Hypothermia was a distinct possibility as he crouched under the tarp in the back of Robert Benton "Little Boy" Kew's Dodge pickup. If Little Boy had known Johnny was there, he'd have brought the kid inside, of course, to warmth.

But he didn't know.

His cell phone chirped, he picked it up, was instructed by Estelle, punched off, started up, and drove away.

With Johnny shivering in the back.

• • •

"How much for da gum?" asked the first goon.

"Ninety-five cents," answered the pimply teen, scratching a wet spot.

"For a pack of gum?" said the second goon.

"You don' like it, don' buy it," said Pimples, still scratching.

Goon Number One considered slapping the pimply punk silly, but resisted the impulse. They were supposed to remain low profile. He put a pair of fins on the counter.

The kid looked at them. "Gee, ten bucks. You want somebody killed?"

Goon Number One closed his eyes and counted to ten. Twice. Then he said, "Just a coupla questions, is all."

Pimples began to pick at a scab on his elbow. "Such as?"

"Dat house down de street, eleven-oh-six, little Cape Cod on da udder side, seen any new kids hanging out dere?"

"Sure. Kid about nine or ten, curly hair, cheap shoes. Name's Eddie something-or-other."

The second goon nodded appreciatively. "He dere now?"

"Well, duh," said Pimples, still picking. "School's been out for an hour."

"Keep the fivers," said Goon Number One, and left.

With the gum.

Leontine Chevalier was on the phone with her sister-in-law, LouAnne. "How long's he been gone," she asked, her stomach in turmoil. "Oh, God, why didn't you call earlier?" she said. "He wouldn't *do* that," she insisted. "Just keep looking," she nearly screamed. "Of course call the police!" she shouted, and hung up.

And then she panicked.

Holmes Crenshaw was trying to calm Leontine by telephone, and having scant success. "No, I don't know how to reach Connor. Did you try his cell phone?"

Then he listened.

"Benella is with you, right?" he asked.

Affirmative from Leontine.

"And she doesn't know where he is?"

That was so, Leontine confirmed. *Nobody* knew where Connor Gibbs was, or so it seemed.

Which wasn't true. Estelle Lawson knew. Little Boy knew.

And so did the short, stocky detective.

LouAnne hadn't been off the phone five minutes when her doorbell rang. *Eddie!* she thought and raced to answer it.

Not Eddie. Two squint-eyed but well-dressed males. "Are you the police?" LouAnne asked.

"You expectin' da police?" answered Goon Number Two, offering his least alarming however snaggle-toothed smile.

"I was hoping maybe . . ." and she trailed off.

"What'sa mattah?" asked the first Goon.

"My nephew Eddie is missing. I haven't seen him since yesterday evening."

"You report it to da police?"

"Not yet."

Goon Number One smiled his most disarming smile. "You have now."

He withdrew from a breast pocket a small piece of paper, wrote a number on it, handed it to LouAnne. "Give us a call should da kid show up. We'll do da same."

LouAnne thanked them and closed the door.

As they descended the stairs, Goon Number Two said, "Do we look like cops?"

"Maybe she was near-sighted," responded his confrère, and they had a good laugh.

To Boz Fangelli, over long distance, from Newark, Goon Number One said, "Somebody's already grabbed da kid."

"That freakin' Helms. What a putz. Sends us on some pussy backup job. Tell Frankie I appreciate it."

"Sure."

• • •

Gantt Helms was watching *Under Siege,* the part where the dancer comes out of the cake, when Slide Websen interrupted.

"What, what?" said Helms, hitting the Pause button. "Now I gotta rewind it. This is the best part." The freeze frame was filled with overdeveloped pulchritude.

Websen had an odd look on his face. "Did you put anyone else on the New Jersey thing?"

"What anyone else? Who'm I gonna put?"

"Boz just phoned. He said his contacts told him that the boy was already gone."

"Whaddya mean gone?"

"Missing. He thinks you went behind him with another team."

"He does, huh?" Gantt stroked his chins. "Well, now, I wonder where the kid is. You suppose his mama sent for him?"

"Who knows?"

"We got someone on Gibbs?"

"Yes."

"Tell him to watch out for a kid, nine or ten, coming or going from the Gibbs place. If they get a chance, grab him."

"Gantt, this isn't New Jersey. This is pretty close to home."

"Just do it!" Helms yelled, and hit Rewind.

Chapter 39

IT WAS AFTER DARK WHEN CAMERON GIBBS landed in Atlanta, beset by guilt. He should have left his mother a note—because she might worry about him. Maybe. So, after deplaning, and with forty-five minutes to spare before departure, he decided to phone.

She was home. And mad. "You used my VISA? And my emergency cash?"

"I had to, Mama. There was no other way to do it."

"Where are you now?"

"I won't say. You'd try to do something to stop me."

"This is exactly the kind of thing your father would—"

"Daddy knows nothing about this! You can't blame him."

"Cameron, tell me where you are so I can make arrangements for you to come straight home."

"No! I just wanted you to know I was . . . okay. So you wouldn't worry."

"You are most emphatically *not* okay. You are who-knows-where, and when you get home, I'm going to—"

"I'M NOT COMING HOME!" he yelled and slammed down the receiver.

Then he sat in a stall in the men's room and cried.

While he was doing so, Felicia Atcheson-Gibbs was dialing her VISA card's 800 number, to trace its last use. Then a call to the airline and she knew Cameron had phoned from Atlanta.

So she alerted the airport police there, and the search for Cameron Gibbs was on.

"Bennie?" said a tearful Cameron. "Is Dad there?"

"Sorry, buddy. What's wrong?"

Cameron told her.

"Your mother will probably trace you to Atlanta before your plane leaves, so don't try to board," cautioned Benella. "Go to a crowded gate and sit near some adults. Try to look as if you're part of the family. When they leave, do it again at another gate, maybe try to strike up a conversation with some kids. Blend. If you see any security people, don't stare at them, and try not to seem nervous.

"I'm coming to get you. When I arrive, I'll have them broadcast a message for Benella Mae Sweet, saying where to meet me. Stay awake, you don't want to miss it. And Cameron."

"Yes?"

"Use your head. You're a runaway, and sometimes there are people in airports who . . . Just stay in or near large groups, and keep your cool. I'll be there in a few hours."

"I'll be waiting," he assured her and rang off.

Swiftly, Bennie left Gibbs a note and was soon spinning rubber down the street in Connor's SVO Mustang. From it she phoned Holmes Crenshaw, asking him to cover Leontine, currently sitting in Connor's kitchen worrying herself sick over Eddie.

"I'll be there in fifteen minutes. Should I call someone in Atlanta?"

"Company people?"

"Sure."

Bennie thought for a moment. "If Cameron does what I

told him, he'll be hard to spot. No, let's leave him to his own devices until I get down there. By the way, I left Connor a note, but you might try to reach him from time to time, in case he has questions."

"Where *is* Connor?"

"He told me he was going to see a man about a dog."

Eddie Chevalier used up all his money taking a cab to his mama's mobile home from the bus station. And now there he was, on his own stoop, with no key and his mama not home. So he went next door to use Mrs. McGuffy's phone. The old lady wasn't there (it was bingo night at church), but he knew where she kept a key.

"Eddie!" shrieked a relieved Leontine Chevalier. "Where are you?"

"At Mrs. McGuffy's."

Through tears of joy, "You stay right there. I'm coming." And she hung up.

But Benella had just left, and Holmes was merely on the way. Who knew when he'd arrive? She had to leave *now;* her son was waiting. So she left Crenshaw a note, scooped up Jared, grabbed her purse (with the gun in it), and called a taxi, praying she had enough money to cover the ride.

She did. Barely. But not enough for the return trip to Connor's. So she and Eddie had a poignant reunion, then went back to their trailer to wait.

For someone to come for them.

Someone did.

Slide Websen, cruising Connor's street, saw something very interesting: a tall, beautiful woman whip out of the Gibbs driveway to go tearing down the street in a hot Mustang. So he pulled into an unoccupied drive within eyeshot, killed his motor, and lit up. Not long after, a big yellow taxi arrived at the Gibbs domicile, and a thin pale woman ran out of the house with a baby and encabbed.

"Hmm," Websen hmm'd, then fell in behind the taxi, singing softly to himself, ". . . big yellow taxi came and took away my old man."

Chapter 40

OUTSIDE CASEY'S DINER WAS A MASSIVE PARKing lot filled with cars and trucks and would-be diners and just-dined departees. Connor Gibbs turned his van into the lot, found a spot as instructed—near the rear and out of the light—and switched off his engine. Nearby loomed a big Dodge Ram; inside its cab was a huge man wearing a snapbrim hat. Gibbs climbed out of his vehicle as the other man quit his, and the two approached.

"Heard a lot about you," Connor said as greeting.

"Heard nothing about you," Little Boy returned. "Except that you don't like dogs."

"I like dogs fine." Connor stuck his hands in his pockets, against the chill.

"I see. It was just Bingo you didn't care for."

"Gantt put that dog on me. It wasn't my doing."

"Gantt didn't break his neck." Little Boy's hands were not in his pockets.

"I understand you know dogs, Mr. Kew. Then you realize that you can't play with an attack dog." He shrugged noncommittally. "I had no choice, like I told you. I'm sorry about the dog, even sorrier that Helms sicced it on me. You'll just have to live with that."

"Whether I like it or not?" said Little Boy, taking a step forward.

"That's right," from Gibbs, hands coming out of his pockets. "And if you take another step, I'm starting this dance."

Little Boy smiled ruefully. "Well, you're tall enough. But do you have the weight?"

"Even if I don't, I have the know-how."

"You want to prove it?"

Gibbs shook his head. "I don't *want* to prove anything. But I can. And will, if you insist."

Little Boy stopped smiling, set his feet, and brought up his hands. Gibbs stepped to one side and brought up his own, just as Johnny Applewhite said, "M-m-mister B-b-boy, I'm f-f-freezing," and fell over the tailgate, headfirst.

Gibbs, very fast on his feet for such a large man, caught the child before his head could hit the tarmac.

Johnny Applewhite was no longer blue, bundled as he was in two very large men's down jackets, and no longer hungry, filled as he was with griddle cakes and mashed potatoes and chicken wings and rich chocolate mousse. He was, in short, as happy as a 'possum in a persimmon tree.

Little Boy, however, was not happy, but his anger had been diverted from Connor Gibbs, now seated in the booth beside Johnny.

"I warned Anson about hitting you," said Little Boy to Johnny. "When I get back, I'm going to tie him into several knots."

Johnny was suddenly apprehensive. "I don't have to go back, do I?"

Little Boy didn't know how to answer that.

"Where are your parents, son?" Connor interjected.

The boy's shoulders slumped. "Gone," he mumbled.

Gibbs looked at Little Boy, who shook his head minutely.

"Is this Anson gent family?" queried Connor.

"An uncle," said Little Boy.

"No other close relatives about?"

Little Boy again shook his head. "None who would take him in."

"How about you?" Connor's eyes searched Little Boy's.

"Yeah," prompted a suddenly revived Johnny Applewhite.

Little Boy shifted nervously. "What would I do with a kid?"

Johnny's face fell.

"Not that I don't like you, Johnny. It's just . . ."

"What?" from Gibbs.

"Yeah, what?" echoed Johnny.

"I'm not exactly a role model."

Gibbs said, "You work for Gantt?"

Little Boy nodded.

"You tied into him on paper?"

Little Boy shook his head.

"Then walk away."

"And do what?" Little Boy wanted to know.

"What can you do besides train dogs to kill each other, grow weed, and paint cars?"

Little Boy's nostrils flared, but he managed to maintain control. "I'm the best mechanic you ever saw."

Johnny chimed in. "He is, too."

"Then be a mechanic," suggested Connor.

"Not easy. I work best on my own, and don't take orders well. Besides, mechanics don't get rich."

"You getting rich working for Gantt?"

"Not rich. But I have some put back."

"Enough to open your own garage?"

Little Boy thought about it. "Maybe, if I could get a building cheap enough. And build a reputation. But Gantt sees to it that I'm left alone, no hassles. I have a cabin, no rent. I get food from Anson's store, up to five hundred a month, no charge. Got two vehicles to drive, cost me nothing."

"How about if you take a fall? Say some Fed stumbles over a grass patch, or you get snagged for switching numbers on a Beemer. Gantt going to jail for you, too?"

Little Boy's eyes smouldered. "You push pretty hard, mister."

"You seem to have a brain, Mr. Kew. Too good a brain to be doing what you're doing. So let me make a prediction. Gantt Helms is going down. And soon. You need to get out now. If not for yourself, for Johnny. Who else has he got?"

Johnny simply stared at Little Boy, the only man ever to stand up for him, show any consideration at all.

"No agency would let me adopt—" Little Boy began.

"What if they would?" Gibbs interrupted. "Or at least appoint you his guardian?"

Johnny's eyes began to fill.

Little Boy noticed the tears, and said, "You know a good lawyer?"

Connor grinned. "It happens that I do, the best in Wendover. And he's cheap."

"A good lawyer that comes cheap?"

"Well, pretty cheap."

"But," asserted Little Boy, "you need to understand a couple things. First, I never had anything to do with Gantt's dog fights. Nothing. Second, I still owe you for Bingo. I nursed that dog back to health once, after the vet said he would never make it. He didn't deserve what you did to him."

"I agree. But what he didn't deserve *more* was Gantt Helms as his master. I said I felt bad about Bingo, but I won't apologize. I did what I had to do."

"And someday I mean to stomp a mudhole in you for it," Little Boy said, eyes like flint.

"After this is over, you're welcome to try. But let's put it on the back burner for now. Deal?" He offered a big hand across the table.

After a moment's hesitation, Little Boy took it, in a hand even bigger than Connor's.

Chapter 41

"WE'RE TRYING TO HAVE DINNER HERE!" GANTT Helms yelled into the phone. He had spaghetti sauce on his shirt and butter on the back of a hand. He licked at the butter as he listened.

"No shit," he said into the mouthpiece. Then, "Now ain't that interesting." Then again, "Well, now." And hung up with a queer look on his face.

"What?" said Sherman, noticing the look.

Gantt sat heavily. "Guess who just had a meeting."

"Tell me."

Gantt bit into a roll, then licked more butter off his hand to go with it. "Little Boy and Gibbs."

"What!"

"My thoughts exactly."

"Where?"

"Over to Casey's. First out in the parking lot, then they went inside. Had a boy with 'em."

"The Chevalier kid? Or that little punk hangs around with Gibbs?"

"Couldn't be sure. Kid had on a big coat." Gantt finished

the roll. As he chewed, the bread distended his left cheek. Sherman looked away in disgust.

And the phone rang.

"We're trying to fucking eat here!" Gantt screamed into the phone. Then, "Yeah?" Then, "No shit." He cupped the receiver in his fat hand and said to Sherman, "Guess where Slide is."

"Just tell me, stop with the guessing games."

"Outside the bimbo's trailer. Guess who's inside."

Sherman shook his head in exasperation.

"The bimbo, with both her brats."

"Nobody else?"

Gantt uncupped the mouthpiece. "Who else is there?"

After getting the response, he said to Sherm, "Slide ain't seen anybody else."

"Then have him go in and get her," Sherman said.

"Round 'em up," Gantt instructed. "Bring 'em to the dump on Route 24." And he slammed down the phone, grinning maliciously.

"Round *them* up. What you want with the kids when you got the woman?"

"I want her to squirm a little, that's what. Nothing makes a woman squirm like hurtin' her kids," he said, burped, then took a third helping of spaghetti.

The rest of the meal passed silently, except for an occasional gastrogenous upheaval.

"Might as well just knock on the door," Slide Websen said to himself. "She doesn't know me from Adam's house cat."

So he knocked.

Leontine Chevalier had just hung up from Holmes Crenshaw, who had promised to come get her and the boys posthaste, when a knock sounded at her door. Eddie was moving to answer it when she hissed at him, held up a warning hand, then withdrew from her purse the Charter Arms

.38. First she checked that it was loaded, then held it down at arm's length beside her, hidden in the folds of her dress. After whispering specific instructions to Eddie, the boy tiptoed to the door, unlocked it, then went to the couch, carefully picked up the sleeping Jared, and retreated down the hall to the master bedroom. Only then did Leontine say, loudly, "Come on in."

Just the thin, pale woman in sight, standing in the center of the living room with no lights on. "Hi," Slide Websen said and reached for the wall switch beside the door.

"Don't touch that," said Leontine.

"It's awfully dark in here," objected Websen, his hand hovering near the switch.

"I can see fine."

"Well I can't," from Websen, his hand moving again.

"You touch that button, and things are gonna go really dark on you. Permanently."

Websen grinned wolfishly. "You going to hit me with an iron?"

Up came the Charter Arms. "No, I'm gonna shoot you like I did them dogs."

Slide Websen believed her, so his hand eased away from the wall.

"Now drop *your* gun," Leontine said.

"I don't carry one."

"Friend, all of Gantt Helms's trash carry guns, and if one don't hit the floor at your feet pretty quick, I'm gonna blow a hole in you." She cocked the gun with her thumb.

"Okay, okay." Websen was suddenly very nervous. "Hey, when you got a gun cocked like that, it doesn't take much for it to go off."

"You are exactly right, and I'm a mite skittish, so I wouldn't be long about tossing your piece."

He did so. It bounced on the worn carpet at her feet.

She said, "Now, go sit in the kitchen," and picked up his gun.

He did.

"Put your hands on the table, where I can watch them."

He did. "Now what?" he said.

She sat on the ottoman. "Now we wait."

Websen was even more nervous. "For what?"

"For you to become impatient. Then I get to shoot you five times."

He sat very still.

"Hello the house," said Holmes Crenshaw, from outside.

"That you, Mr. Crenshaw?"

"Indeed it is, Ms. Chevalier."

"Come in slowly. There'll be a man to your right, seated at my kitchen table. Don't get between us. I plan to shoot him if he makes the smallest move."

"Wouldn't want to interfere with that," Holmes answered. "Here I come."

"What's your name, mac?" said Leontine.

"Websen."

"Mr. Crenshaw, meet Mr. Websen."

Holmes displayed a mouthful of perfect teeth. "How do. You'll pardon me for not shaking hands, but that would put me in the line of fire, and Ms. Chevalier seems pretty anxious to shoot you."

Sweat broke out on Slide Websen's forehead.

"I called the po-leece on the way over, Mr. Websen," Holmes allowed. "They should be here any time."

Sweat broke out on Slide Websen's upper lip.

"Of course, you don't have to be here when they arrive."

In Slide Websen's eyes, a ray of hope.

"Assault, B&E, attempted kidnapping, attempted rape, sitting in the dark. Got lots of stuff on you, Mr. Websen."

"So what do you want from me?"

"Tell me everything I need to know to put Gantt Helms away. And brother Sherm."

"If the cops are on the way, we don't have enough time."

"Maybe I was kidding about the cops."

"Were you?"

"Sure. But I can still call them."

"No need. But would you have her decock that revolver? It makes me nervous. She's had it pointed at me for ten minutes. She must be getting tired."

From beneath his suit jacket, Holmes drew a handgun of his own and pointed it at Websen. "Okay, ma'am. You can put yours away."

She did, and Websen began to talk.

After two minutes, Holmes produced a tape recorder, and turned it on.

Braxton Chiles, standing on Leontine's stoop, said, "Barrister Crenshaw, how are you?"

"Fine as frog hair, Mr. Chiles."

Chiles dipped his head to Leontine, then said, "Slide."

Websen said nothing.

"Mr. Websen and I had a meeting of the minds," Holmes informed, "and he decided to provide me with a lengthy transcript, now complete. However, and not to put too fine a point on it, I do not fully trust Mr. Websen. I wonder if you would, pro bono of course, impress it upon him just how important it would be for him to seek calmer climes, ASAP."

"Pro bono?"

"Well, there was that Georgia thing."

"Right. Sure, I'll speak with Slide, even let him hitch a ride home."

Websen said, "That won't be necess—"

"Sure it will," Crenshaw cut him off. "Ms. Chevalier needs a car, what with hers being in the shop and all, and your new Chrysler will do fine. Won't it, Ms. Chevalier?"

"I've always had a thing for Chryslers," Leontine agreed.

"See? It's settled. You ride home with Mr. Chiles, here, probably in the trunk would be best, and toss a few personal items in a suitcase. Then none of us will ever see you again, will we?"

Websen shook his head.

"Well bye," from Holmes, as he went to the refrigerator.

"By the way," said Braxton Chiles as he was leaving. "I've been looking for Connor. Do you know where I can reach him?"

Pouring milk, Holmes said, "Not at the moment. But I'll give him the message. Thanks for your help on this."

And that was that.

"You're not really going to put me in the trunk?" said an incredulous Slide Websen.

"It needs to look good, doesn't it?"

"Shit," Websen complained and climbed in.

Braxton Chiles drove for nearly two hours, to an abandoned mine shaft near Unionville, where he stopped to release Websen from the trunk.

"What the fuck!" shouted Slide as he clambored out of the back. "I was in there forever!"

"No," said Chiles, "but you will be in *there* forever." And pointed a finger.

When Websen turned to look, Braxton shot him in the left temple with a small-caliber pistol, to avoid making a mess. For such a slight man, Braxton Chiles was very strong. He had little trouble carrying Slide's inert body into the shaft, then dumping it down a very deep hole.

The body is probably still there. What's left of it.

Chapter 42

OVER THE PUBLIC ADDRESS SYSTEM AT ATLANTA International Airport blared the message, "Ms. Benella Mae Sweet, please meet your party at Gate 22." It took Cameron Gibbs nearly eight minutes to get there. But get there he did, unimpeded, where Benella scooped him up in her long arms. Cameron was delighted, and envied by every male within eyeshot.

After leaving the airport, Benella said, "You hungry, big guy?"

"Ravenous."

She laughed deep in her throat. "You talk like your dad."

So they found a Denny's, and put away enough food for three. But first they called Connor. When he answered, Benella said, "I've got him."

Gibbs sighed deeply. "Any baggage?"

"No, and I've doubled back on myself twice. No one behind us."

"May I speak with him, please?"

Bennie relinquished the DCS phone. "Daddy?" said Cameron Gibbs.

"Son, this was not the smartest thing you ever did. But I'm glad you did it."

"You are?"

"At the moment. After your mother trots out her big guns, it'll remain to be seen. How are you?"

"Hungry enough to eat a manatee."

The elder Gibbs chuckled. "Hide and all?"

"You bet."

"You didn't eat at the airport?"

"I was too scared to move, almost."

"Nothing on the plane?"

"All the peanuts I could munch, as long as it was only two bags. And a Coke. I stashed one bag of nuts. It was supper."

"Resourceful. You take after your godfather, the inestimable Mr. Crenshaw."

"No, sir. I take after my daddy."

After a moment to swallow the sudden lump in his throat, Connor said, "Be safe. I love you, son."

"Love you, Daddy."

Denny's was looming.

Connor and Holmes and Leontine, sitting in the Gibbs den, late, sharing the events of the evening. Holmes was saying, "You really believe that Little Boy will turn his back on Gantt?"

"Maybe. I noted some sense of loyalty, but not an overwhelming one. And then there's the question of Johnny. Mr. Kew seemed genuinely concerned. That boy could be the difference," Connor reasoned.

Leontine said, "So with the Websen slug out of the picture, who else do we have to worry about?"

"I'm not sure," from Gibbs. "I'll get in touch with Braxton, see who's left on the active payroll."

"That reminds me," Holmes said, "Chiles said he'd been looking for you. Don't know why."

"I'll give him a buzz in the morning. Meanwhile, are you planning to take Websen's tape to the DA, or do you need to, ah, edit it?"

"I'll listen to it a time or two, then decide. If good old Gantt will just lay low for a day or so, we should be able to spring a surprise on him."

Woulda, shoulda, coulda.

Before Connor went to bed, Estelle Lawson called.

"You still in one piece, studly?" she asked.

"Such confidence in me."

"I have all the confidence in the world in you. It's just . . ."

"Just what?"

"Bobby-B is . . . sort of in a class by himself."

"Never laid a finger on me."

"Then you didn't meet with him."

"In fact, I did, and we smoked the pipe of peace. For the moment. Events are escalating, things are fomenting."

"He didn't smack you upside the head. For Bingo?"

"Not yet, but we discussed it. He settled for a rain check."

"Keep me posted."

"You'll be the last to know."

"That's what I'm afraid of. By the way, my partner has a real hard-on for you, and he's the sneaky type."

"Keep an eye on him for me."

"Can't. He took a couple days off. Personal leave."

"If I run into him, I'll give him your regards."

She kissed Gibbs good-bye over the phone.

Little Boy checked himself and Johnny into a Motel Six, then spent most of the night wrestling with his conscience.

Johnny slept just fine, thanks. For the first time in months.

Next morning, the incongruous pair had a big breakfast, and went to see Gantt Helms.

•   •   •

"The boy stays with me," rumbled Little Boy.

Marvin, the former marine dog handler, responded, "That's not what Mr. Helms said."

"It's what I say."

The former marine dog handler shrugged, tilted his hairless pate, and said, "Follow me."

And to the pool they went. Where Gantt waited. And Sherman. And where Choi, the houseboy, was serving up frosted Bud Lights, and where the Jewel, newly brushed and radiant, lay on a thick purple velveteen pillow, alert and implacable, her intelligent eyes fixed on Little Boy Kew.

There were no empty chairs around the pool, so without preamble, Little Boy said, "Get up, Sherman."

Sherman said, "What?"

And Little Boy said, "I told you to get up. I'm not going to stand while Gantt sits."

Sherman looked at his brother, who was indulging himself with a small smile. "Whatever you want to do," Gantt said to Sherman. "It makes no difference to me."

So Sherman stood, shifting his weight nervously from one foot to the other, while the vacated deck chair creaked in acceptance of Little Boy's bulk.

Gantt said, "Comfy?"

And Little Boy said, "One thing before we start, Gantt. If that dog comes for me, or the boy, I'll take her into the pool. You know what'll happen then."

Gantt's indulgence disappeared. "You'd drown her."

"Easily. Even the boy could."

Gantt's piggy eyes nearly closed. "First Websen, now you."

"What about Websen?"

"Who the fuck knows? Last night he was going in after the bimbo and her kids. This morning, no word. Go figure. Whaddya want?"

"I'm serving notice."

"Notice? You think this is a fucking union shop?"

"Figured I owed you. I'm going back to Jefferson, turn the books over to Pepper, if he'll take them. He might not. Either way, I'm gone."

"By when?"

"Tomorrow."

Gantt snorted derisively. "Not much of a notice."

And Little Boy said, "Better than none at all."

"What if I decide you know too much about my operation to let you walk?"

"Nothing you can do about it."

"I could have you snuffed."

"Yeah? Who's gonna do that for you?" Little Boy's head came around toward Sherman. "Him?"

"Not that he couldn't, but no, not him. No need for you to go back west, Little Boy. Sherm'll administer the switchover. You stay the hell away."

"I've got some things—"

"YOU GOT NOTHING! Whatever's in that cabin belongs to me! You go up there and I'll have you shot, you oversized lump of camel shit!"

Little Boy stood. "I'm going, like I said. If you or anyone working for you tries to stop me from taking what's mine . . ."

Gantt sneered. "What'll you do?"

Little Boy said nothing else.

"See?" Gantt addressed Sherman. "He's all brawn, no balls. You can go now, chump. Take the orphan with you."

And Little Boy left, with Johnny.

During all this dissension, the Jewel never took her eyes off Little Boy.

Sherman said, "Things are falling apart, brother Gantt."

"Send Marvin in here," Gantt said.

"Marvin's a schmuck."

"HE'S A FORMER MARINE!"

"Give up on this, Gantt."

"FUCK YOU! SEND ME MARVIN!"

Sherman shook his head in frustration. "You're crazy," he declared, and left.

Subsequent events proved him correct.

"Choi, take the rest of the week off. Go visit your family in Greensboro," Sherman instructed.

"Sir?" from a befuddled Choi.

"Don't come back before Monday, no matter what. And take your personal stuff."

"I don't understand, sir."

"You will. And Choi?"

"Yes, sir?"

"You've done a helluva job." Sherman passed the Vietnamese an envelope. It contained three thousand dollars, cash, and a green card.

Choi had never had a green card, let alone three thousand dollars in cash. He left immediately.

Sherman never saw him again.

Sherman had gathered several bank books, bound together by thick rubber bands, and three checkbooks. On his way out of the house, he found Marvin washing one of the Mercedes. "Gantt wants you," Sherman told Marvin. "But I wouldn't do a thing he says, if I were you."

A thoroughly perplexed Marvin hustled in to see his boss.

That was too bad.

Thirty minutes later, Marvin was off to do a job en route to Jefferson.

That was even worse.

Chapter 43

CONNOR AND CAMERON HAD BEEN SEQUESTERED in the study for nearly an hour, plotting a strategem, when Blister McGraw phoned, wanting to know if he could come over. Connor said sure, do you need a ride and Blister said no, Aunt Vera will drop me off, and so it went.

Alas, Blister never arrived.

Former marine dog handler Marvin Strupp had never been overloaded with gray matter, and to him one ten-year-old kid pretty well looked like another, so when Vera McGraw dropped Blister at the bottom of Connor's driveway and departed, Marvin popped up from the bushes, grabbed the boy, chloroformed him, hoisted him over a shoulder, and hiked off through the neighborhood, quite proud of himself.

Prematurely.

"That's not the Chevalier kid," said Manning, the dirty cop, bending over to examine Blister, asleep on Gantt's sofa.

"So who is it?" questioned Sherman, newly cash-heavy after six trips to various banks, unbeknownst to brother Gantt.

"I think it's the McGraw kid, the one that hangs with Gibbs sometimes," Manning suggested.

"Will he do us any good?" Gantt asked.

Manning shook his head. "Can't see how."

"But who the hell knows?" Gantt mused. "Tie him up and stick him in the basement. We'll see how it plays out."

So Marvin took Blister to the basement, bound him hand and foot, blindfolded the boy, then continued on to Jefferson.

As I said, Marvin was not especially smart.

"Blister should have been here by now," Connor opined.

"Maybe his aunt decided against letting him come over," Leontine said.

"Maybe, but he would have called."

Just then the phone rang. When Connor picked it up, Braxton Chiles said, "Mr. Gibbs."

"Mr. Chiles. I hear you've been trying to reach me."

"Indeed, my man. I've something for you. Can you come by the warehouse?"

"Now?"

"When convenient. I'll be here all day."

"I was expecting Blister, but he's running late."

"It would be best for you to come alone."

"All right. How about an hour from now?"

"Perfect."

After he'd hung up, Connor said, "Leontine, Bennie and Cameron will stay here with you and the boys. Stay inside. When Blister shows, call me on my mobile."

At the door, Benella took Connor's arm. "You heeled?"

"I'm just going to see Braxton."

But she was worried. "Things are sort of coming to a head here, and Helms troubles me. Not to mention Little Boy."

"If things get worse, I'll stick a gun in my belt. Not now, though. It'll chafe."

And out the door he slipped.

Little Boy, with Johnny beside him on the seat, cell-phoned Pepper and requested a meet at Little Boy's cabin. Pepper agreed, unfortunately.

Chapter 44

AFTER CLEANING OUT HIS BANK ACCOUNT AND safe-deposit box, and picking up a few items from a storage facility held in a fictitious name, Little Boy and Johnny stopped at Anson's store. Uncle Anson was not delighted to see them.

"I need you to write me a letter," Little Boy told Anson Applewhite.

"Kinda letter?"

"Saying that Johnny is coming to live with me for a while."

"Huh? How long a while?"

"'Til you're dead or he's grown," growled Little Boy.

"Won't be worth the paper it's wrote on," Anson objected, until his wife came over.

"Do the letter," she said.

Anson did the letter.

Braxton Chiles's warehouse was short on parking space, so Connor had to park two blocks away and go shank's mare. Outside a sliding steel door, he pulled a cord, which prompted a ring deep within.

From a squawk box, a scratchy voice. "Identify."

"W. C. Fields."

"That you, Mr. Gibbs?"

"Here I stand."

A buzzer sounded, and the steel door slid open.

Connor Gibbs walked in, and the door slid solidly shut behind him. Down a narrow corridor, and into the brightly lit office earlier described. Behind one of the desks sat Braxton Chiles, splendid in a short-sleeved Hawaiian shirt and string tie.

He held a .45 automatic.

At Little Boy's cabin, near Jefferson, Pepperoy Jenesais-Quoi was saying, "I train dogs to fight, an honorable profession. I do not peddle the dope, nor steal and market automobiles. Dogs only, for me. You must get Yip to do this."

"Yip's too dumb to pour piss out of a boot, Pepper. You know that."

"Then Mr. Helms has a big problem," insisted Pepperoy.

"I suppose you're right. You liquid?"

"What is liquid?"

"Is your money where you can get at it?"

Pepper sniffed disdainfully. "Of course."

"Then I recommend you get at it. Gantt's house of cards is about to come down," Little Boy said, just as Yip walked in.

"How you hanging, Little Boy?" was Yip's salutation.

Little Boy never had a chance to answer.

"That the new SIG compact .45?" Connor asked Braxton Chiles.

"It is."

"Any count?"

"SIGs used to have a great single-action pull, and a mediocre-to-lousy double-action. These new ones have a mediocre single-action and a horrible DA. Is that progress?"

Chiles dropped the magazine from the SIG, jacked open the slide to show that it was unloaded, and handed it to Gibbs.

While Connor was examining the gun, Chiles said, "I guess you've heard that Websen is history."

Connor nodded as he tested the SIG's action.

"Are you also aware that Marvin Strupp has been sicced on Little Boy?"

"Who's Marvin Strupp?"

"Ex-marine, takes care of that big dog of Gantt's. Runs errands."

"I wouldn't classify Little Boy as an 'errand.' "

"No, but Little Boy isn't a shooter. He likes to work with his hands."

Connor handed the SIG back to Chiles, who poked the loaded magazine back into its opening and snapped the slide forward to chamber a cartridge.

Gibbs said, "And this Marvin is a shooter?"

"If I were going after Bobby Kew, I certainly would be," said Chiles and stuck the SIG under his shirt. "Though admittedly a missile would be preferable. By the way . . ."

Chiles opened a drawer, withdrew a thick envelope, and tossed it to Gibbs. "Merry Christmas."

Connor examined the contents: five thousand in cash. He raised a quizzical brow.

Chiles was smiling happily. "That's your half of ten grand, a down payment on your life. The deal was for forty more on completion."

"Gantt?"

Braxton nodded.

"You accepted his offer?"

Still smiling, "Of course."

"You gave him your word?"

"What's that Ernest Borgnine line from *The Wild Bunch*? 'It ain't your word, it's who you give it to.' "

"Thanks, Mr. Chiles. Half this will go to Leontine, the other to a boy named Johnny."

Chiles dipped his chin in response. "Better get the word to Little Boy, before it's too late."

But it was already too late.

Former Marine Gunnery Sergeant Marvin Quincy Strupp was no rocket scientist, as has been previously illustrated, and he was somewhat short of tactical skills. He had hidden himself near the doorway to Little Boy's cabin, behind a clump of mountain laurel, and had been trying to work up sufficient nerve to burst in and start blasting when a propitious opening presented itself, in the form of Yip Cantrell, now coming up the walk to the front of the cabin. In behind Yip did Marvin slip, his Uzi at the ready.

When Bobby Kew, alias Little Boy, heard Yip enter the cabin, he glanced up. Not only had Yip come through the front door, but some jazzbo in a camo outfit was right behind him. Said jazzbo immediately whipped out a machine pistol and opened fire, with the first ten or so shots nearly ripping poor Yip in two. Pepperoy dove behind a cedar chest as Little Boy yelled to Johnny, "Into the bathroom! Go out the window!" which advice young Johnny followed quickly and to the letter. As Johnny was quitting the scene, Little Boy scrambled behind a heavy oak desk and scrunched up, as much as a 285-pound man *can* scrunch up. Meanwhile, Sergeant Marvin—fearful someone might be ready to pop up with a gun and shoot *back*—finished emptying his thirty-round magazine as a preemptory move, then kicked out the window nearest him and dove through it. His awkward landing knocked the now-impotent Uzi from his grasp and the wind from his lungs. Flight beckoned, so he took the opportunity.

Johnny Applewhite was the scaredest he'd ever been, but his allegiance to Little Boy was strong. So he sneaked around the front of the cabin just in time to see (and hear) Marvin

Strupp make his hasty exit, drop the Uzi, then stumble off toward the garage. Johnny went in to tell Little Boy.

"Pepper?" yelled Little Boy.

"*Sacre bleu!*" breathed Pepperoy.

"You okay?"

"Except for my pantaloons, which are filled to the brim."

"Little Boy!" shouted Johnny, bursting through the front door.

"Over here. Why didn't you run?"

"I wouldn't leave you. Anyway, that man dropped his gun and ran down to the garage."

That was all Little Boy needed to hear.

Well crap, Marvin Strupp thought to himself. *Not only did I drop my gun, but now I got Goliath to deal with. I'm in for it.*

He was pretty much correct.

Little Boy's phone rang. It was Estelle. "Who is this?" she asked when Pepper hello'd.

"Who wants to know?" Pepper asked back.

"I'm Essie Lawson, a friend of Little Boy's."

"I have heard of you. I am Pepper, also a friend to Little Boy."

"Is he there?"

"At the moment he is occupied."

"Please tell him that a man may be coming to kill him."

"*Now* you call us," said Pepperoy Jenesais-Quoi.

Little Boy came through the door like a huge gymnast, executing a neat shoulder roll on the concrete and fetching up behind an air compressor. "Friend?" he said.

Marvin did not answer.

"Oh, friend?"

Still nothing from Marvin, who was busy trying to swallow.

"If you won't talk to me, we can't work this out."

"Work what out?" Marvin croaked.

"Your blowing my pal Yip into several parts."

"No negotiations. You can just let me out of here."

"Afraid not. I wasn't especially fond of old Yip, but his mother probably was."

"*Probably* was?"

"I never met her."

Out came Marvin's Buck knife, its edge like a razor. "I've enjoyed this conversation, but I'm going out, around you or through you," Marvin said, and stood up.

So did Little Boy, between the former sergeant and the door. "Reckon it'll have to be through me."

To give Marvin his due, he tried very hard, and for, oh, ten seconds, it was touch and go.

Then Little Boy touched him *real* hard, and Marvin went.

"Is he dead?" asked Pepper Jenesais-Quoi.

"If he ain't, he's gonna have one hell of a crick in his neck," said an awestruck Johnny Applewhite.

"Are the police on the way?" from Little Boy.

"I called them," said Johnny. "Poor Yip."

"Then I'll wait," said Little Boy.

"And I," said Pepper. "You will need as many witnesses as possible. Then tomorrow, I will head north. With dogs. Gantt Helms does not deserve them. He is a *salope*."

"Whatever that means," Little Boy whispered to Johnny.

And they waited for the police.

Chapter 45

THREE DAYS BEFORE CHRISTMAS, EARLY EVENING, light snow and carolers in front of Vera McGraw's house. She'd worked late and was not in a good mood, and the semi-messy condition of the house did not bring a bloom to her cheeks. Nor did the snow, nor the stupid singers, now deep into "Carol of the Bells."

Vera hated Christmas. Too many memories, none of them good. She fixed coffee, ate two cold biscuits with cold country ham, and picked up the phone.

"Hello," said Connor Gibbs.

"You're doing all right, I trust," said Vera McGraw.

"Not bad, and you?"

"Tired, irritable, premenstrual."

"Same as always, then."

"You bet. Put Cody on, will you?"

Instant alert on Connor's end. "He isn't here."

"What do you mean he isn't there? I dropped him off this morning."

"When?"

"Right before work. He called to see if it was okay." Vera was becoming alarmed.

"I know, I spoke to him. But he never showed. I assumed you had changed your mind."

Very alarmed now. "No, I dropped him at the end of your drive on my way to work."

Connor's heart skipped a beat. "Hold on, this may take a minute," and he set down the phone. "Bennie! Cameron!" he shouted, and they came running.

It was Cameron who found the tracks, behind the largest mimosa, and called to his dad. In less than a minute, Gibbs was back on the phone with Vera, explaining the situation.

She nearly fainted from fear.

"The pace is seriously accelerating," Gibbs informed Holmes, who was working late at his office.

"You call the police, or the FBI?"

"No. I considered it, but if Helms has him—and who else would?—who knows what he might do?"

"I concur. I'll be there in twenty minutes, and we'll decide how to play this."

"What's that all about?" the short, stocky detective asked himself when two large adults and one child came running out of the Gibbs residence to cast about like hunting hounds. Within minutes, they'd gathered in one spot, near the corner of the house, then run back inside.

He had the car window open, so snow could fall on his hair. He liked snow. He bit into a tangerine and waited.

"You going to Shoo Lin's?" Sherman asked Gantt.

"Hell, yes. This weather's not keeping me in," from Gantt, tugging on his rubbers.

"Who's driving you?"

Gantt tossed Sherm a look. "Me, myself, and I, smart ass. You coming?"

"Think I'll stick by the phone. We haven't heard from Marvin."

"He'll call. You oughta come eat some pork-fried rice."

"I'll be okay."

"Choi's gone off somewhere, the chink bastard. You'll have to do your own cooking."

"I'll be okay," Sherman insisted.

So his brother tossed up his pudgy hands and left.

As soon as Sherm heard the Mercedes leave the drive, he grabbed a few things and went down to the basement.

Cody Wainwright "Blister" McGraw had been very disturbed, not to mention scared, when he awoke bound like a Christmas goose. And *blindfolded* yet. At first, he'd yelled and kicked, but then figured that since only the kidnappers were likely to hear him, his tantrum would have limited value. So he'd started crying. But not long, after deciding that (a) sobbing like a baby probably wouldn't free his hands and feet and (b) he wouldn't give his tormentors the satisfaction of knowing they'd made him cry. So he quit. And lay still. For a very long time.

Now he was hungry, and he was even more frightened, and he *had to pee . . .*

Abruptly, a door opened, well above him and to the rear. He feigned sleep.

Sherman Helms flipped the basement light switch before descending the stairs; he wasn't about to break his frigging neck. Standing on the bottom step, he whispered, so as to disguise his voice, "I know you ain't asleep, kid. And I hope you ain't dead, 'cause I'm taking you outa here."

Then he crossed the floor, applied chloroform to a washcloth, and the cloth to the boy's face for a short while, then lifted the unconscious form, carried it up the stairwell, carefully stuffed it into the boot of the smaller Mercedes, climbed behind the wheel, and drove off.

"Now what we got?" the thickset detective said to himself, as the Mercedes slowed to a stop and its driver quit the seat, opened the trunk, and dumped a bundle into the yard. The driver got back into the car, found reverse, and backed down the street and out of sight. The short, stocky dick never got a make on the plate.

But he did note that the bundle moved, slightly. So he went to investigate. After all, he was a cop, off duty or no.

"Missing something?" said the squat homicide detective as he stood on Connor's stoop, arms full of Blister.

"Connor," said a weak, cold Cody McGraw and held out his small hands.

Gibbs had him in a second.

Vera snatched up the phone at its first jangle. "Cody!" she sobbed, then listened briefly. Then, "I'll be right there!"

And in fifteen minutes, she was.

Sherman was watching brother Gantt the way a chicken eyes a fox. They were out by the pool, with the Jewel on her royal pillow, and Gantt was an unhappy camper. He paced back and forth, both hands behind his broad back.

Sherman was saying, "We don't make war on kids, brother."

"He was our ace in the hole!" argued Gantt.

"We'll have to make do. I'll have nothing to do with stealing kids."

Gantt's head jerked around at Sherman's tone. So did the Jewel's. Sherman fingered the pistol hidden beneath his leg as he sat. It didn't reassure him much.

"Sherm," said Gantt Helms. "Seems that ever'body has either quit on me, or been killed. The TV says that Marvin bought it up in Jefferson, and Websen ain't been heard from, and Sam and Junior went south. Mo and Iggy fell down on the job, Little Boy turned on me, and prob'ly Pepper, too. Even my slope housekeeper's turned up gone. But what hurts the worst is you skulking around behind my back."

"I wasn't skulking. You just weren't here when I made up my mind."

"Hear that?" Gantt said to the Jewel. She looked at him, then back at Sherman.

"Well, brother," Gantt continued. "I guess I better go it alone from here. You take that pissy little Merc and get as far away from me as you can, and stay that way. We're quits, you and me."

"I'm due some big dough, Gantt. And I want it."

"Your wants could get you killed." Gantt Helms turned his whole body, slowly, to face his brother. The Jewel picked up on the vibes and stood, bristling.

Sherman produced the gun from underneath his leg, saying, "If she even growls, I'll shoot her right between her stupid eyes."

Gantt's right hand came out from behind his back. There was a revolver in it. "And I'll shoot you right between yours."

So Sherman backed away, and through a swinging glass door, then hoofed it quickly out of the house and into the small Mercedes, already packed in anticipation of just such an exodus. He was whistling a tune from *Annie, Get Your Gun* when he rotated the ignition key and blew himself to pieces.

"I hope you remembered to get the money out of the trunk before you wired the car."

Nod of confirmation.

"Where is it?" Gantt asked.

"In you bedroom. Two suitcase."

Gantt nodded. "Good work. Oh, and I'll want the green card back."

Choi's black eyes glinted. "I think I keep."

Gantt stared hard for a second, then dismissed the subject. "What the fuck," he said, and dove into the pool. The resulting splash hit Jewel in the face. She never blinked.

Chapter 46

CONNOR AND CAMERON GIBBS, BENELLA MAE Sweet, Blister and Vera McGraw, Holmes Crenshaw, Leontine and Eddie Chevalier, and Estelle Lawson and her partner, the short, stocky detective, were gathered in the Gibbs living room. Baby Jared was upstairs in his crib, half asleep and sucking his middle and index fingers. Downstairs, the TV held everyone's attention, because on the screen Gantt Helms was raving to a reporter.

"It was that BLEEPing Connor Gibbs!" ranted Helms.

"But sir, you can't be certain of that," the reporter objected.

"The BLEEPing BLEEP I can't, him or that BLEEPing bimbo who hired him, the one who BLEEPing threatened to kill me, right here on this BLEEPing television station, in front of every-BLEEPing-body in the state!"

"Sir, if you'll calm down a minute, I'd like to ask—"

"CALM DOWN! How the BLEEP can I calm down when my brother has just been exploded like a BLEEPing pomegranate!"

"May I turn that off?" asked Vera.

Connor handed her the remote, and Vera hit Mute, then said, "I still think we should call the FBI."

"We discussed that already," from Estelle. "What do we tell them, Vera? No one saw anything. Blister—"

"Cody!" snapped Vera.

". . . *Cody* doesn't remember anything except being grabbed, then waking up tied and blindfolded. Forensics could go over the abduction site, but it's pretty well snow-covered. Besides, based on Connor's assessment of the boot tracks he found, it was probably that ex-soldier boy of Gantt's, now residing in a Jefferson morgue."

"Remember," Crenshaw put in. "Our diligent district attorney is sitting up late playing and replaying the tape I so thoughtfully supplied her. She'll check some things, recheck some things, and when she's ready, send some uniforms over to see ol' Gantt. But she'll wait 'til she's sure of a sky-high bail, so Gantt won't simply post it and skip to Guatemala."

"Guatemala?" Connor said.

"Just an example," Holmes said.

Connor chewed his lip in remembrance. "I know . . . but do you remember that Easter airdrop—"

"Oh, *please*," from an exasperated Vera. "No war stories. Now isn't the time."

Benella Mae looked at Vera. "Why not? We're in full-wait mode. Besides, I'd like to hear it."

Eddie said, "Me, too."

"Go on, Dad," Cameron agreed.

So Connor told his war story. Cold war, that is.

"Thanks again," Vera told the short, thick dick, "for bringing Cody back to me."

The detective said, "Just lucky I was watching the house, lady, no big deal."

When the two cops left, Estelle said, on the way to the car, "By the way, why were you watching the house? You were supposed to be off for a couple of days, or so I thought."

"I was on my own time, and I didn't trust Gibbs. Now I do. No problem."

They piled into their car and left, with Estelle still bending his ear.

"Leontine?"

"What?"

"We've got too many kids around," said Connor. They were in the kitchen preparing cocoa.

"What do you mean?"

"Helms already snared one. You think he's above going after another?"

"But they're all with us."

"We don't know how many troops Gantt may bring in from the outside. Sure his local staff is depleted, and his brother gone—I wonder who was behind that—and Little Boy is out of the picture for the moment, but all it takes is money to hire creeps. Gantt has plenty of that."

"He needs to be put under," said Leontine.

"Abandon that sad refrain. He might not get put under, but he's going to be put *away*, and for quite a while. Then your life can go back to normal. Be satisfied with that."

I'll be satisfied when he's dead, thought Leontine, but what she said was: "So what about the kids?"

"I've been working on that. Holmes is going to spend a few days at Vera's, to cover Blister. He's got no court cases this close to Christmas, so his hardship will be minimal."

"You call living under one roof with that woman minimal hardship? Over Christmas?"

"It was his call, though Bennie volunteered. But I preferred that she take Cameron to my dad's mountain cabin, with Dad going along. That way I have plausible deniability of Cameron's whereabouts when Felicia points the authorities at me."

"Does she know he's here?"

"Only that he is safe and not in Atlanta. He called her from a cell phone."

"Was she pissed?"

"My understanding is that she redefined the word 'pissed.' "

"You didn't talk to her?"

"No. Cameron, then Bennie."

Leontine chuckled. "She intimidate Benella?"

"Bennie is, ah, not easily intimidated."

"But Felicia tried."

"Of course."

"So what'd Benella do?"

"Laughed at her."

"Laughed at her?"

"And then hung up."

Leontine grinned. "I'd like to have heard both ends of that conversation."

Connor handed her two cups, steaming and filled. She took them to Cameron and Blister. "Here, *Blister,*" she said, looking directly at Vera as she handed the boy his cocoa. Vera thinned her lips and looked away.

Back in the kitchen, Connor said, "We can keep both of your boys here, but covering them will be harder than if one or both of them were out of the area."

Leontine thought a moment. "Can't you send Eddie with Cameron?"

"I suppose I could, but I'd prefer not to have two eggs in one basket."

She thought some more, but came up with zero. "What do you suggest?"

"Either send Eddie to a relative far away, or let me ask Braxton Chiles to babysit."

"How about Abernathy?"

"Well, there'd be plenty of kids for Eddie to play with, but he wouldn't be as safe. Besides, it might bring trouble to the Abernathy household, and that kind of trouble is not his thing."

"So Chiles is your best bet?"

"His warehouse is a fortress. And a labyrinth. If Hitler'd had a place like that, he'd be alive and well."

"But very old."

Connor grinned and handed her two more steaming cups. "I could ask Estelle if she might take a couple days off. Otherwise, she'd have to leave Eddie alone when she went to work."

Leontine took the cocoa into the living room, giving one to Eddie, the other to Holmes. She looked pointedly past Vera McGraw, and said to Benella, "Would you like some cocoa?"

Bennie smiled and demured. "Got to watch the waistline."

Blister McGraw, long smitten by Benella Mae, said, "As if you had one."

"When you're of age," Bennie said with a soft smile, "I might marry you."

Blister blushed. Cameron saw it and couldn't resist twisting the knife. "When'll he be of age?"

"A year or so," Benella answered, and everyone laughed. Except Vera.

Once again in the kitchen, Leontine declared, "Jared will stay with me."

Gibbs nodded. "I figured. You and I will watch out for him."

"We've done okay so far."

"You bet."

And so it came to pass that on the morning of Christmas Eve Cameron Gibbs departed with his grandfather and Benella Mae Sweet for a secluded mountain safehouse; Holmes Crenshaw settled into the McGraw extra bedroom, no TV, but with a copy of Wilton Barnhardt's *Gospel*; and

Eddie Chevalier kissed his mother good-bye on Connor's stoop and climbed into a '40 Ford coupe with Thorton Chiles, Braxton's younger brother.

Now all the children were out of harm's way.

Except Jared.

Chapter 47

Robert Benton "Bobby-Kew" "Bobby-B" "Little Boy" Kew had been released on his own recognizance, pending a final hearing, which would undoubtedly find for justifiable homicide, or self-defense, or rodent extermination, and was currently and rapidly en route to Wendover with Johnny Applewhite asleep at his side, leaning against the big man's massive right arm as Little Boy piloted his Dodge Ram V8, which occasionally broke traction on the snowy mountain road. Mr. Kew's jaw was set determinedly, since he had a king-sized grievance to settle with Gantt Helms, Esq.

"Wow, what a place!" an excited Cameron Clayton Gibbs said to his grandfather, Walter Clayton Gibbs, Jr.

"Not bad for a refurbished hunting camp," Walter beamed.

"What's refurbished, Paw-Paw?"

"Redone, refinished."

"Did you do it?" from the grand-scion, as he bounced on a big four-poster bed.

"Me and Benella here."

Bennie was unloading provisions onto the kitchen counter.

"No kidding? Bennie, did you help?"

"Sort of. What he isn't telling you is that I did most of the work."

Walter harrumphed. "Just the electrical. And the plumbing. And most of the carpentry. But I set those stones outside, at the front edge of the porch."

"The walkway?"

"Yep. All my doing," Walter allowed.

Benella just smiled and began to shelve the comestibles.

"Breakfast, Mr. Crenshaw."

"Holmes, son. Just Holmes."

"Aunt Vera says I'm to call you Mr. Crenshaw."

Sotto voce, Holmes said, "Your aunt got something against black folks, son?"

"No, just *men*folks."

"Oh. I'll try to keep out of her way, then."

"That's wise," said Cody Wainwright McGraw. "It's what I do."

And the two broke their fast together.

Pop-Tarts.

Blueberry.

No frosting.

And no coffee.

The hardships had begun.

"What shall we do today, Mr. Gibbs?"

"Stay in, pray for some real snow, maybe play cards, enjoy Mannheim Steamroller, wrap some gifts, watch one of the *Home Alone* movies, or *Scrooged* maybe, or the Albert Finney version of *A Christmas Carol.* Drink eggnog—"

"Take a long, hot bath?" suggested Leontine.

"Not together."

"That's in the past. I know you've got Benella, and I like her."

"Me too."

"Duh. Well, I'm going up to check on Jared. If he's still down, I'll hop in the tub. Wake me in an hour."

"No need. If he frets, I'll tend to him."

"I'll hold you to that," said Leontine and went to bathe.

Peace reigned . . .

Outside, a small band of carolers, despite the early hour, and two toddlers trying to do snow angels in the minuscule blanket of snow, and a lone man, young, dressed not unlike a Jehovah's witness, riding a bicycle, obviously going about the Lord's business . . .

They did not all look alike, despite the cliché, and thus he recognized that the first out was the Gibbs child, well protected by a tall old man with a gun under his sweater and a woman as big as Norway but with less body fat. (The McGraw child had left the night before, and there had been no point in taking that one again . . .)

Ah, the Chevalier youngster, for certain, and accompanied by only one, and a boy at that. How simple . . .

He cycled to his Honda, dumped the bike (not his to begin with), and followed the ugly old Ford at a discreet distance. When they stopped at a signal, he lightly rear-ended the old car, and as expected, the boy driver popped out as if from a toaster, and the two argued for perhaps five seconds, until a simple knife hand to the larynx ended the conversation.

The boy in the car was even easier; a simple display of the dagger and the child climbed free of the car, walked stiffly back to the Honda, eased himself onto its front passenger seat, then waited, petrified, as Choi walked around back, slid beneath the steering wheel, and engaged the clutch.

Away they went.

Chapter 48

"MR. GIBBS," THE VOICE CAME OVER CONNOR'S cell phone.

"What's up?"

"This is Braxton."

The hair at the base of Connor's neck ran amuck.

"What is it?"

"I'm at the hospital. My brother's here, with a crushed larynx. It was touch and go for a while. He's sedated now."

"What happened?"

"He was struck in the throat. We have no clue by whom. Obviously, he can't tell us."

"I'm sorry. Is Eddie okay?"

"Eddie wasn't with him."

Connor's face lost all expression.

At that moment, Connor's land line rang. Leontine was coming down the stairs, enrobed, drying her hair with a huge blue towel. He could smell her from twenty feet away. "Get the phone?" he snarled. Noting his gravity, she said "sure" and light-footed it into the kitchen.

And then her face lost all expression.

• • •

"Who's this, the bimbo?"

"Who's this, the man whose ass I'm soon gonna shoot off."

"You'll get your chance. Wanta speak to your son?"

The breath caught in her throat.

And then Eddie was on the line. "Mama?" He'd been crying, unusual for Eddie.

"Don't worry, baby. I'll come for you."

"But they—"

"Hey, bitch?" Helms again.

"Speaking."

"Want the kid back?"

"Just tell me how you want to do this."

So he told her. At the conclusion, he reminded, "Remember, no cops, no six-foot bimbos from hell, not that nigger lawyer, either, and especially no fucking *Gibbs*. You unnerstand?"

"Oh, you bet. Me and you, Fatso. Finally. Just one thing, though. I'm not coming to your house."

"You don't, I'll feed the kid to my dog."

She held her breath for a moment, then pressed her bluff. "You plan to do that anyway. Look, I said I'd meet you, and just the two of us, but not on your home turf. And not 'til I know Eddie will be safe. So you come up with a trade, or I take my chances on what you'll do to my son and call in the Feds, right now."

Gantt thought a minute. "Okay. Here's how we'll do it." He was finishing his instructions when Gibbs came into the room. Leontine listened intently, as white as a ghost.

On the phone to Holmes Crenshaw, Connor was saying, "It's going down tonight."

"I can't let you do this alone."

"No choice. Besides, we have no idea how many players Gantt has. If something goes wrong, Eddie's dead, make no mistake. So we'll play Gantt's way, at least until the exchange."

"Who's making the exchange? Obviously not Gantt."

"I have no idea."

"Well, shit, *Sufi.*"

"Right on, Holmie. You just cover Blister, you hear?"

"What about Jared?"

"I called Estelle. She's coming here to stay with him."
Holmes hesitated. "This stinks, buddy."

"Indeed. You hang tight, I'll call when it's over."

"Watch your back."

"You bet," Connor promised.

But he didn't.

On a yellow pad, Thorton Chiles, drugged but still in pain, and having great difficulty breathing, wrote:

Asian guy Five-six, 220-240 40±. Very fast Never saw it coming Bumped me at a light I

Braxton took the pen, then the pad. "Not to worry, he's good as dead," he whispered. "You sleep now."

Thorton nodded almost imperceptibly and closed his eyes.

Braxton said to the cop guarding the door. "I don't know you, and you don't know me. I don't think he's in much danger at this time. But if he is, and you let someone get to him, your pension will go uncollected. Catch my drift?"

The cop, a sturdy third-generation German, said, "I'm not used to being threatened."

"I don't give a shit what you're used to, just do your job," Braxton concluded, and walked away.

"Tell us one more time," Gibbs told Leontine.

To Connor and Braxton Chiles, on stools in the Gibbs kitchen, Leontine reiterated: "Connor goes to the mall and, in the south entrance, walks halfway to the end of that corridor, near Belk, and waits. He'll see Eddie, and it will be obvious what to do next."

She looked at Gibbs. "Once you have him, you call me on your DCS phone, so it can't be monitored, and tell me you have him. I'll be at another location, and Gantt will be close by. He'll tell me what to do then."

"It stinks. I won't be there to help you, Leontine," Connor objected.

"Of course not, but he wants me, not you. The important thing is for you to get Eddie."

"It'll just be you and Gantt." Chiles stated the obvious.

"The way I've always wanted it."

"Mr. Chiles here could follow you, at a distance—" Connor began.

"No. If Gantt spots anyone near me, he said he would call someone who'll be watching Eddie, and . . . No, let's do it Gantt's way."

"What time?"

"Five to six. The mall closes at six on Christmas eve. Most of the shoppers will have left by that time."

So Connor said okay, and Chiles said he was going back to the hospital, and Leontine went to feed Jared.

At 5:22, Estelle Lawson rang the doorbell. Connor filled her in.

"Connor, this sucks," over the phone.

"Bennie?"

"This *really* sucks."

"Now Bennie."

"Don't 'Now Bennie' me! This whole thing sucks, and you know it."

"We have no choice."

"Put it off, let me get back down there and cover your ass."

"Then who covers Cameron's?"

"Walter. He has a Galil and three mags."

"Bennie, Dad means well, but he isn't you."

"But sugar pie," she whined. "All the action's where you are, not up here in the flapping Blue Ridge."

"So far as you know. He could just be trying to draw you away."

"Nobody followed us here. Don't you think I made certain of that?"

"Of course. But the cabin is registered in Dad's name. Helms has a network of—"

"Okay, okay. Just watch your back, you hear me!"

"I will," he lied again, and hung up.

"Where's Braxton?" Estelle asked.

"The hospital. I understand Thorton's in pretty bad shape."

Estelle went up on her toes to kiss Connor on the cheek. "Be careful, you big lug."

"You just take care of Jared."

"And Connor?"

"Don't tell me to watch my back."

"Get out of here," she grinned at him. And to Leontine she said, "Good luck."

Leontine smiled and preceded Connor out the door.

"You have your gun?" Gibbs asked as he helped Leontine into the van. She nodded in return.

So he went to drop her off.

At this point in the festivities, Connor didn't expect a tail, so he didn't spot one. Nevertheless, a dark green Buick followed him all the way to the mall after he dropped Leontine at a taxi stand.

The Buick hung well back, to prevent detection, though its driver didn't really care if he lost sight of the Gibbs car. After all, he knew where Gibbs was going.

Chapter 49

LITTLE BOY DIDN'T HAVE A GUN—HE DIDN'T LIKE them—but he did have a machete in his hand as he negotiated the huge house. Funny, no alarm. And no watch dogs, nor booby traps, nor trip wires. Not even a water balloon wedged in a door to fall on his head. No nothing, in fact. No Gantt Helms, no Sherman, no Choi, no Danny Manning, no Slide Websen.

And no Jewel.

"I know it's Christmas eve, but where is everybody?" Little Boy mumbled to himself.

After covering the entire house, he hustled back to where Johnny waited in the Dodge, and motored away.

One snip and that was that.

Connor Gibbs had no landline.

Gibbs was halfway to the mall when he remembered something. He picked up his cell phone and dialed.

Busy.

Five minutes later, still busy.

So he tried another number.

● ● ●

"Damn, Estelle!" said the out-of-breath short, stocky detective.

Estelle stood in Connor's open doorway. "What?"

"Didn't you realize Gibbs might need to reach you?"

"Yeah, so?"

"Then why have you been on the phone all night?"

"I haven't . . ." She turned abruptly, walked hurriedly to the hall phone, picked up the receiver. "Dead as spats," she said.

"Gibbs needs you right now. At the mall."

"Why?"

"He didn't tell me, just said he'd been trying to reach you and he needs you there, like right now."

"Shit!" from Stelle. "How can I go, I've got the baby?"

"That's why he phoned me. I'll stay with the kid while you go see what Gibbs wants."

"Will you do that?"

"Sure. I ain't saying I want to swap spit with Gibbs or anything, but hey, if he takes Helms out, some of the credit might fall on me and you, y'know?"

Estelle snatched up her purse and coat, saying, "I just fed the baby and put him down. He should sleep for three or four hours unless he has a BM."

"No problem, Estelle. You think I don't have kids?"

"Right." She jerked up her keys and raced to the door.

The driver of the green Buick had no trouble keeping the Gibbs vehicle in sight, since the mall parking lot was pretty empty; obviously most folks had given up on shopping and gone home with their families. *Where I should be,* thought the driver. The Gibbs van stopped outside the southern mall entrance, sat for a moment with lights on, then suddenly went dark.

Then Connor Gibbs got out, apparently prepared to run the gauntlet.

Chapter 50

CONNOR ENTERED THE MALL EXACTLY LIKE JOHN Wayne entered the saloon at the climax of *The Shootist*—full of cocky bravado, or at least appearing to be, the better to intimidate whoever was watching. And someone *was* watching, Gibbs was sure of that. As his long strides took him toward the entrance to Belk, as instructed, his gaze took in everything: three teenagers to his right, outside a jewelry store, arguing about a necklace; to his left front, the obligatory Salvation Army Santa, slowly ringing a handbell, silently pleading for one last-minute contribution, but looking as if he didn't expect to get it; an elderly couple sitting on a wrought-iron bench eating ice cream, two spoons and one cup; a group of merchants, locking down a storefront and discussing the day's receipts; Eddie Chevalier, on a bench by himself, directly in front of Belk, staring straight ahead, not looking at Gibbs or anyone else, simply staring, as if drugged, his steepled fingers in his lap, his coat folded neatly beside him. And that was the extent of the tableau, at least within a twenty-yard radius—no one else moved, or lurked, or appeared to be observing . . .

. . . So Connor walked directly to Eddie, whose eyes still

did not find his, and stopped in front of him, until Eddie's eyes finally moved, not to look at Connor, but past him, *behind* him . . .

. . . And Gibbs started to spin toward the swishing sound of cloth against cloth, light footwork on tile, but too late, and too slow, and a searing pain entered his back, plunged deep into his chest, and he turned anyway, bringing around a heavy arm to ward off, but his attacker went under it and slashed again, and blood—*Connor's* blood—spurted red and plenteous, spraying a scarlet wash all over Eddie and the old couple and Santa Claus . . .

. . . and Connor bellowed his rage and frustration and impotence and went down . . .

Chapter 51

IT WAS DARK ON THE GOLF COURSE, AND THE wind was picking up, and a cold, cold rain was drifting down, as Leontine slogged her way toward the fourteenth hole, a par 3, 210-yarder. Two-thirds of the way to the green, a huge oak divided the fairway, its leafless arms spreading skyward magnanimously. She stood beneath it, as instructed. Five minutes. Ten. The wind was actually beginning to howl, or at least to whistle ominously.

He's doing this on purpose, Leontine, she thought. *Just to spook you. So don't let him do it.*

She glanced at her watch: 6:40. Distant street lamps gave some illumination, but not much. She tried humming to keep her spirits up. Didn't work. She flipped up her collar against the wind, immediately dumping water down her back.

That was brilliant, she chided herself, and looked at her watch again: 6:41.

Walking around the tree, and back again: 6:43. Reverse direction: still 6:43. She closed her eyes and counted to three, backward from 100.

Hey, 6:45. Time's flying.

So around the tree over and over, clockwise first, then counter. The exercise didn't seem to help against the cold; she was starting to shiver. She did some squats, thrusting her arms out for balance. After forty, she was rubber-legged. She sluiced around the oak some more, even walking backward once. *I'll hit my head on a limb,* she told herself, and abandoned the walking backward.

She paced ten yards straight out from the base of the oak, then retraced her steps. Then went a quarter of the way around and paced out from that side. And back. Another quarter-rotation and pace. Then back. Again, and she'd covered all quadrants. Her watch said 7:01, and Gantt Helms said, "Well, well, the woman who wants to kill me."

Chapter 52

BRAXTON CHILES ENTERED THE MALL JUST IN TIME to see Santa Claus stab Connor Gibbs in the back, then duck as Gibbs tried to defend, then cut again, and again, until Gibbs jumped out of reach, tripped over a bench, and went down, with Santa in hot pursuit, slashing left-right-left, until Eddie Chevalier, full of ginger and spunk threw his coat over Santa's head, enraging the less-than-jolly old elf, who for a moment turned his attention to the boy, the knife flashing, tossing glints of refracted light as the child scrambled in terror, with Santa right behind, until Gibbs, crimson and irate, bellowed like a bull and charged Santa from behind, enfolding him into his great arms then flinging him more than twenty feet through the air, away from Eddie but close to the elderly couple, and the deranged Santa gave the old lady a hack as Braxton was running the length of the corridor screaming *"HEEEEYYYYY!"* as a distraction, and when Santa's face came around—smooth and slender and oriental, beardless, now, from exertion—Braxton shot him through the left eye, and suddenly there was even more blood, bright, arterial . . .

. . . Final.

Chapter 53

"AND I *AM* GOING TO KILL YOU, HELMS," LEON-
tine said. "Tonight."

"Maybe so, maybe not," Helms retorted. He was standing
thirty yards away, at the edge of the rough, framed by
stunted elms in the background. To his left front was an
amorphous four-legged mass, resolutely implacable, thick
and malignant and terrifying. "By the way," he continued,
"sorry I'm late. I had a phone call. You know how it is."

"No problem. I was enjoying the scenery. Never spent
much time on a golf course."

Helms came closer, halving the distance. "By the way, I
have a surprise for you," he said, the wind plastering his
soggy hair to his head. "Sort of a family reunion."

Her mind suddenly in turmoil, Leontine started to speak,
but a voice stopped her, somewhere off in the distance.
"Gantt?"

"Over here," Helms yelled, turning his head toward the
voice.

"And in less than a minute, to this dreary scene was an additional player added.

Two, actually.

"Danny Manning, you know Leontine Chevalier, of course," said Gantt Helms.

The short, stocky detective had a bundle in his arms, but it was too dark for Leontine to make out what it was. "Sure," said Manning. "Hiya, Mrs. Chevalier. Recognize this little guy?"

And he whipped off the blanket and held Jared up for all to see.

Chapter 54

Estelle Lawson was well on her way when she heard the emergency call over the police band; all available officers were ordered to report to the mall, shots had been fired, multiple citizens down, carnage everywhere. She lit up her roof and floored the gas. By the time she arrived, a dozen squad cars and four ambulances were stacked outside the south mall entrance like cordwood. She parked and ran inside, flashing her badge. Pandemonium reigned. She spotted Connor being rolled onto a stretcher. Gibbs was beside himself as she hurried up to him. "Stelle, Eddie's safe! You have to call Leontine so she can break off the meet! Here's her cell phone number!" and he fished a small paper from his pocket, despite an IV attached to his arm. "Quickly! It was scheduled for 6:30!" Estelle looked at her watch: 6:27. So she jerked out her phone and punched in the number Connor had given her . . .

"The cellular customer you are trying to reach is either out of range, or . . ."

Chapter 55

LEONTINE CHEVALIER'S HEART WENT STONE COLD when she heard Jared's first cry of anger and discomfort as the freezing rain hit the baby in the face. She gripped the gun in her right pocket like a lifeline. Which it was, more or less. Only a gun could save her and her baby now, and she knew it.

"Listen to him yell," laughed Gantt. "He's pretty pissed at you, Manning."

Manning shook the screaming baby. "Hey, quiet kid. Can't you take a little bad weather?"

The Jewel, silent until now, growled deep in her throat. Because Leontine was striding closer, determinedly, both hands in her pockets as if from the cold and damp. Her eyes were dead.

"Whoa, lady," warned Gantt. "The Jewel doesn't like you too close."

"I blew the fucking brains out of two of your mutts, Gantt. If she moves, I'll blow hers out, too." Then she turned her attention to Danny Manning. "Put the baby down."

Manning just laughed in her face, as Jared screamed and the Jewel growled.

Helms said, "Go ahead."

"What?" from Manning.

"Go put him under the tree, there. Maybe he won't get so wet, and he'll shut his yap."

"I'll walk with you," Leontine said.

"We'll all go," insisted Helms. "Jewel, heel."

So they all walked to the ancient oak, and what a pitiful procession for such an exclusive golf course: a sopping wet, rogue cop carrying a screeching, equally soggy baby, both followed by a thin, pale woman seemingly too feeble even to resist the wind, all trailed by a fat man and his monster dog, and probably none of them members.

Manning plopped the wailing Jared in the mud at the base of the giant oak and straightened up. When he had done so, Leontine drew her Charter Arms .38 and shot him in the side of the neck, whereupon he began to cough and hack and spit up blood and tissue, and to spin in a frantic circle until he had spun five or six times, then sat down and rolled over on one side. Meanwhile Leontine turned the gun on Gantt Helms, or tried to, but the Jewel had charged as Leontine was gunning Manning, and when she turned to shoot Helms, the dog closed her jaws on Leontine's shooting wrist and bit down HARD, crunching both the lower arm bones and several of the wrist, but Leontine pulled yet another gun from a rain-soaked pocket and stuck it against the Jewel's snout. That would have been that had not Helms seen it and shoved Leontine's hand away in the nick of time, deflecting her bullet into the tree, from which bark flew, and then yelled "*Jewel, off!*" and the Jewel desisted immediately, and backed away to stand near the bawling baby, as Leontine dropped one gun, due to her mangled arm, and brought the second to bear on Gantt, finally, but too slow, since he saw it coming and knocked it from her grasp with a big fat fist. Leontine, gunless, hit Gantt in the throat with a pretty good straight left, which was not pleasant for him, then raked his jowls with her clawed fingers, nails bared, drawing both blood and a yowl of pain that rivaled Jared's irate cries. Next she went for his piggy eyes, but he hit her a right cross, or his best attempt at one, and knocked her against the tree. When Gantt moved in to finish the woman off, she saw him coming and kicked him on the point of his knee, very HARD, which sent his temper over the top. He grabbed her slender body at the hips, spun his corpulent, pain-racked self in a half-circle, lifting her from the ground as he did so, and whacked her against the trunk of the oak like a ball bat, her head impacting with a sickly THWOPP! Her thin body went loose, but not entirely so, so Helms repeated the move, spinning like a hammer thrower to bash her head once more into the tree.

And she was dead.

And Gantt knew it.

But so enraged was he, that her actual death wasn't enough. He needed to *punish* her! So he kicked her lifeless body, again and again, over and over, for nearly a minute, screaming at the top of his lungs all the while, "FEEL GOOD? FEEL GOOD?" And still he was not vented. He wanted to punish her MORE! But how . . . as the baby's cries filtered through his anger.

"Shut up!" he yelled at the child.

Jared did not.

"SHUT UP!" Helms screeched insanely.

Jared did not.

"I said SHUT UP!" from Gantt Helms, now completely out of control.

Jared did not.

"I'LL STOMP YOU INTO THE GROUND!" hollered Helms, and went to do it.

Chapter 56

"WE HAVE TO FIND HER, STELLE! WE HAVE TO. She's on her own." Connor Gibbs, still covered with his own blood, lay strapped into the back of an ambulance as its sirens wailed.

It was 7:14, and Leontine Chevalier was not "on her own." She was dead. And little Jared was well on his way to joining her, but neither Connor nor Estelle could know that.

In the speeding ambulance, Estelle said, "Who shot Santa?"

Connor shook his head.

Estelle said, "Who *was* Santa?"

"Gantt's houseboy."

"So where's Eddie?"

"Safe."

"Connor. I need to know what went on tonight."

"Officially, or unofficially?" He winced in pain.

"You put me in a very awkward position, here."

"Make up your mind. These drugs are starting to take effect."

"Okay, unofficial. Quick, tell me."

He did.

She didn't like any of it.

Chapter 57

THE JEWEL GROWLED DEEP IN HER THROAT AS Jared lay screaming beside her.

Gantt Helms stopped in his tracks at the sound of the growl, absolutely incredulous. "WHO DO YOU THINK YOU'RE GROWLING AT!" he yelled, rain pelting his face.

The Jewel remained still, but stopped growling.

Jared did not stop screaming.

Gantt took a step toward the child.

The Jewel took a step toward Gantt, and growled again.

"What the fuck? Listen, dog, you better move the hell outa my way!"

The Jewel took another step, placing herself between Helms and the baby.

"I SAID MOVE, YOU ROTTEN FLEABAG!" Helms screamed hoarsely, and started to take another threatening step.

The Jewel growled deep, deep within her being.

Gantt Helms was too angry to notice.

"MOVE!" he yelled, and kicked the Jewel.

A major mistake.

As soon as Gantt's foot connected with the Jewel's nose,

she clamped down on it, twisting her huge head to one side. Down went Helms, landing on Leontine Chevalier's battered body. Suddenly, Helms kicked again, lashing out with his right foot.

The Jewel ignored the slashing foot, fending it off with a shrug.

Then went for Gantt's groin.

Sharp canines sank into Helms at the juncture of his thighs. One of those canines perforated the femoral artery, high, near the scrotum. He screamed in horror and anguish as his scrotal sac was ripped away. Then the Jewel once again sank her teeth in.

This time for good.

He weakly pummeled her head for many long, agonized minutes, as he lay writhing on his back, kicking, squealing like a shoat.

To no avail.

The Jewel held on.

And on.

Until her master had bled to death and the baby had stopped crying.

Then she let go of Helms's genitals, or what remained, trotted to the supine and passive baby boy, gently picked him up by his sleeper, and carried him to the groundskeeper's shack.

Fortunately, the groundskeeper was not drunk at the time. But soon he was very sick.

Later, he got drunk.

And swore never again to spend Christmas Eve avoiding his family.

Chapter 58

ON CHRISTMAS DAY, BENELLA MAE WAS BED-side, and Connor Gibbs was bedridden. But, considering that some blear-witted worm within the anonymous confines of his HMO did not feel a collapsed lung and multiple knife wounds warranted more than an overnight stay in the hospital, the bed was in Connor's home.

Cameron was at the Gibbs residence for Christmas Day for the first time in two years. Due to the extraordinary efforts of Bennie and Estelle, who somehow had found an open store catering to the yuletide needs of ten-year-old boys (mostly electronic, or at least battery-powered), he was happy, and at this mid-day moment was plotting, along with Holmes Crenshaw, their fend-off-Mom-and-her-bloodthirsty-attorney strategy. (Cameron would swear to a judge that he would simply run away from home *again* if denied frequent access to his dad, specifically through visitation.)

Vera McGraw and Blister were also present at the Gibbs household, both in the kitchen preparing gustatory delights for the upcoming Christmas feast.

Eddie and Jared Chevalier unfortunately were still in hospital, Jared with a mild case of pneumonia, Eddie heavily sedated and under observation. The older boy had not yet been told about his mother.

"Are Leontine's boys going back to Jersey?" Benella was asking Connor.

"I suppose they'll go to whoever will take them. Leontine didn't have any insurance, not even a burial plot, but Gantt Helms left a sizable estate, not all of it forfeitable to the authorities. I'm sure Holmes will sue on behalf of the boys, and for a good chunk. They were, after all, orphaned by Gantt."

"Gantt have family to fight for the money?"

"I have no idea."

Walter Gibbs came to the master bedroom door. "Son?"

"Don't 'son' me. You have no idea how many men Mother knew."

"I base my supposition on certain physical characteristics that we share."

"Such as?" Gibbs said to his dad, who had the exact same eyes, hair, nose, and was within a half-inch in height.

"We each have a mole."

"Where?"

"Yours is on your left elbow."

"Where's yours?"

"Never you mind."

"You base paternity on such flimsy evidence."

"Well, I did, ah, bed your mother once, and at about the right time, ten months before you were born."

"*Ten* months?"

"You were always a late bloomer."

"What do you want?"

"There's a man to see you. Has a kid with him."

"The man large?"

"About two ax handles across the shoulders."

"That's Little Boy."

"Of course it is."

"Would you show him in, please, oh pater, dear?"

Walter Gibbs looked at Bennie. "Did I rear him to be that way?"

"He always told me he was raised by wolves," Benella asserted.

"Close. Coyotes," Walter said, and went to fetch Little Boy and Johnny Applewhite.

Little Boy said, "How are you?"

"I've cut myself worse shaving," said Gibbs.

"Right," said Bobby Kew and shifted from one foot to another. "You had this deal pegged pretty close. About Helms, I mean."

Gibbs nodded.

"Still don't like what you did to Bingo."

"Neither do I."

"Just wanted to touch base with you. Johnny and Pepper and I are headed north. All the way north."

"Good luck to you. Did you talk to Holmes Crenshaw about the boy?"

"I did. He says he'll take care of it."

"If that's what he said, that's what he'll do."

Little Boy offered a hand, and Connor shook it. Weakly. "You take care," said Robert Benton Kew, and then left.

"Are you glad you didn't have to fight him?" from Benella after Little Boy had gone.

"Sure. I didn't want to hurt him."

They both smiled at that.

"What now?" Gibbs pretended pique.

"Another male visitor," said Walter from the doorway. "This one a bit smaller."

"Look like Woody Allen?"

"I suppose, if Woody Allen were a hangman. By the way . . ." He hesitated.

"Yes?"

"He has a, um, bouquet about him, a certain . . . pungence."

"Braxton Chiles," Bennie and Connor said in unison.

"Should I ask him up, or to bathe first?"

"Just don't insult him. He saved my bacon, Pop."

"Then I have something else to hold against him," Walter quipped, and went for Chiles.

"Your father?" asked Braxton Chiles, tossing a thumb at the departing Gibbs.

"So he claims."

"There is an amazing resemblance."

"And we each have moles."

"I beg your pardon?"

"Never mind." Gibbs held out a hand. "You saved my hide, Braxton. And likely Eddie's as well. Choi had things going pretty much his way, for a while there."

"I was affronted by his disguise. I give generously to the Salvation Army each year. They do important work."

"So, if he'd been dressed as Frosty the Snowman, I'd have been in trouble?"

Braxton simply shrugged.

"How's Thorton?" questioned Gibbs.

"Better. They'll send him home tomorrow, most likely. He's in pain, though."

"I'm sorry. He was helping me."

"Hey, you're worse for wear as well, my man."

"Any word on that lady Choi gashed?"

"Sewed her up and sent her home. To Bridgeport. Little Christmas excitement Down South. It'll serve her well at her next coffee klatch."

Walter appeared in the doorway. "Estelle Lawson just drove up," he announced to the room at large.

"That's my cue. Me and the police seldom mix. Later, my man. Have a joyous Noel." And Braxton Chiles faded away.

• • •

"What a mess," greeted Estelle Lawson.

"Why aren't you home?" Connor bussed her cheek.

"Alone, on Christmas? Thanks a lot."

"No siblings? Aunts, uncles, cousins, ne'er-do-well nephews?"

"Spare me. I have a raft of relatives, none of whom I would spend three seconds with voluntarily, especially at Christmas."

"Then you'll dine with us," Benella offered.

"Twist my arm." Estelle smiled, then shifted gears. "Who'd a 'thunk that Danny Manning . . ."

"Don't beat yourself up, Stelle. Manning was the one playing both ends from the middle, not you."

"Well, he sure had me fooled."

"By the way," Gibbs asked, "whatever happened to Gantt's dog, the one that saved Jared?"

"It's in the pound."

"Not to be destroyed, I hope. I mean, the dog's a hero. She carried Jared to safety."

"What, you want to adopt the dog, you big palooka?" from Estelle.

Gibbs just shrugged, and the trio spent a desultory half hour until Walter called them to table. With Bennie's strong arms assisting, Connor made it okay, despite his recently perforated lung. He ate pretty well, too.

In the pound, so did the Jewel.

After all, it was Christmas.

Epilogue

CONNOR AND CAMERON, ALONE TOGETHER, FIRST time all day. They sat on the big leather sofa, watching the lights on the tree, some strings blinking on and off, some just shining festively. At the foot of the tree, mounds of gifts, all opened, the paper scattered.

"How was your Christmas, son? You get enough stuff?"

Cameron was sitting on a cushion and leaning his head against his dad's shoulder. "Being with you is enough. I didn't need presents. But it would have hurt Bennie's feelings if I hadn't acted excited."

"And Stelle's."

"Right."

"And Paw-Paw's."

Cameron grinned sleepily. "Um-hmm."

"Did you remember to call your mom?"

"Yes."

"Did she wish you Merry Christmas."

"No. She said when I got home . . ."

Well, that was Felicia. Threats, always threats.

"Did you wish her Merry Christmas?" Connor asked, knowing the answer.

"Just as soon as she picked up the phone."

They both sighed. Felicia would never change.

"Let's sing some carols," Cameron suggested, insistent on uplifting the moment.

"Starting with?" From Connor.

And so they sang, father and son, their physical selves so often separated by a continent, but their hearts, now and always, one. The strains of "It Came upon a Midnight Clear" floated down the hall, joyfully brisk. Walter, in the den with a toddy, added his baritone, and three generations of Gibbs men celebrated the birth of a child.

PENGUIN PUTNAM INC.
Online

Your Internet gateway to a virtual environment with
hundreds of entertaining and enlightening books
from Penguin Putnam Inc.

*While you're there, get the latest buzz on
the best authors and books around—*

Tom Clancy, Patricia Cornwell, W.E.B. Griffin,
Nora Roberts, William Gibson, Robin Cook,
Brian Jacques, Catherine Coulter, Stephen King,
Jacquelyn Mitchard, and many more!

**Penguin Putnam Online is located at
http://www.penguinputnam.com**

PENGUIN PUTNAM NEWS

Every month you'll get an inside look at our upcoming books and new features on our site. This is an
ongoing effort to provide you with the most
up-to-date information about
our books and authors.

**Subscribe to Penguin Putnam News at
http://www.penguinputnam.com/ClubPPI**